NOT A TRACE

Praise for Norah McClintock

"John Grisham for teens."
— *Vancouver Sun*

Truth and Lies
" . . . the second book in what one can only hope
will be a multibook series."
— *The Globe and Mail*

Scared to Death
"Buckle up — it's going to be a scary ride."
— *St. Catharines Standard*

"McClintock delivers the goods."
— *Quill & Quire*

Over the Edge
"McClintock . . . delivers a solid mystery. . . . True
McClintock fans will grab a can of pop and gulp
down both story and soda in one nervous sitting."
— *Quill & Quire*

Double Cross
"The climax is fraught with danger and emotion,
and the conclusion is a satisfying end
to a good read."
— *Canadian Materials*

"Lots of suspicious behaviour . . . with a smart,
likeable heroine."
— *Canadian Materials*

NOT A TRACE

Norah McClintock

Scholastic Canada Ltd.

Toronto New York London Auckland Sydney
Mexico City New Delhi Hong Kong Buenos Aires

Scholastic Canada Ltd.
175 Hillmount Road, Markham, Ontario, Canada L6C 1Z7

Scholastic Inc.
555 Broadway, New York, NY 10012, USA

Scholastic Australia Pty Limited
PO Box 579, Gosford, NSW 2250, Australia

Scholastic New Zealand Limited
Private Bag 94407, Greenmount, Auckland, New Zealand

Scholastic Ltd.
Villiers House, Clarendon Avenue, Leamington Spa,
Warwickshire CV32 5PR, UK

Library and Archives Canada Cataloguing in Publication

McClintock, Norah
        Not a trace / Norah McClintock.

(A Chloe and Levesque mystery)
ISBN 0-439-95760-5

I. Title. II. Series: McClintock, Norah   Chloe and Levesque mystery.

PS8575.C62N68 2005   jC813'.54   C2005-900596-3

6 5 4 3 2 1   Printed in Canada   05 06 07 08 09

To JRC and RAZ. Still believin'.

chapter 1

Nearly two months before I found the body in the park, David Mitchell came to my school. From everything I'd heard about him, I thought he would be a lot older, a lot bigger, and a lot more intimidating. I realized later that I'd thought these things because of the way people talked about him. Most people said he was hard, stubborn, confrontational and single-minded. There were some people who had a different opinion, but they seemed to be in the minority.

He came to my school at the request of Mr. Lawry, my history teacher, to give his perspective on an issue that was raging in different parts of the country: First Nations access to natural resources. On the east coast, there had almost been open warfare when the Supreme Court upheld the right of native people to fish out of season. In other areas, non-native loggers who were already struggling with unemployment and idle mills were outraged when natives won the right to log on Crown land.

David Mitchell turned out to be younger than I expected — I guessed he was in his early thirties — and looked to be of average height standing up at the front of the classroom in jeans, a denim jacket and cowboy boots. He wore his black hair long and loose. When he talked, his dark eyes moved from person to person, lingering for a few seconds each time so that,

1

for those few seconds, it was as if he were speaking right to you alone. Some kids squirmed under the intensity of his gaze. Some looked away. I did neither.

At the conclusion of David Mitchell's presentation, when Mr. Lawry said, "Questions?" nobody said a word. Mr. Lawry looked pointedly at me, probably because I have a reputation for talking back to and even arguing with teachers. His thinking seemed to be that I should have no trouble coming up with something to say to a controversial guest speaker. I sighed and stuck up my hand. David Mitchell zeroed in on it.

My question: "Many species, like Atlantic cod, are already over-fished practically to the point of extinction, and we're losing old-growth forest at a rate that's contributing to climate change. How is it going to help if we give more people the right to fish and log? Isn't that only going to speed up the destruction of our environment?"

For a moment, David Mitchell just stared at me. I thought he was annoyed or even angry, but he wasn't. He said he didn't agree with my conclusion. He said it wasn't simply a question of more fishers and more loggers. He said there also had to be serious action on the preservation of our fish stocks and forests, and that we needed sustainable development so that these valuable resources would continue to provide livelihoods for our children and grandchildren. He said we needed fairness, so that all people — native and non-native — could enjoy the fruits of the land. It sounded good until Rick

Antonio — who, go figure, had picked that exact moment to finally pay attention to something that was going on in class — stuck up his hand and said, "So, let me get this straight. Are you saying it's fair to burn the boats of fishermen who are only defending their right to feed their families? Is that what you Indians mean by fair?"

That's when David Mitchell said — and everyone heard him say — that native people had to defend their rights "by any means necessary." Boy, did that wake up the class.

Sarah Moran said, "But some of those means, like burning people's boats, are illegal."

Someone else — I think it was Tim Duggan — said he'd heard there had been bomb threats over access to fish. He said that sounded like terror tactics.

Soon the whole class was buzzing. David Mitchell just stood there, looking and listening. When everyone finally settled down, he reached up and pulled down the map of the world that hung like a window blind above the blackboard. Then he picked up a pointer in his left hand and, tapping various parts of the map, proceeded to give what he called a two-minute history lesson on Aboriginal peoples, which boiled down to: white people have practised genocide on Aboriginal peoples all over the world for centuries; governments have not always been quick to defend native rights; and, to survive, Aboriginal peoples have to be prepared to take matters into their own hands.

The bell rang.

We were dismissed.

I was on my way out of the classroom when David Mitchell stepped in front of me. He was taller up close than he had appeared from halfway back in the classroom. He looked strong and well muscled too, and held himself with the confidence of a guy who wasn't afraid of anything. He said, "Thanks for getting the ball rolling. Gerry said I'd be able to count on you." I wondered what else Gerry Lawry, my history teacher, had said about me to David Mitchell.

"No problem," I said. When he moved aside to let me pass, I hesitated. A lot of what he had said made sense, but there was one thing that bothered me.

"Can I ask you something?" I said.

"Shoot."

"When you say that native people have to be ready to defend their rights by any means necessary, you don't really mean that, do you? I mean, protests, sure. Even a little civil disobedience." His eyes flashed. Okay, so maybe I should have said a *lot* of civil disobedience. "But you wouldn't actually use *any* means, would you? For example, you wouldn't kill anyone. Would you?"

He didn't say anything. Instead he looked at me and I looked straight back, and the longer I looked, the more I thought I saw the answer. Until nearly two months later, when I made the front page of the local newspaper, which happened one week before I found the body.

4

How I got my picture on the front page of the *East Hastings Beacon* is this:

I walked out of the drugstore on Centre Street, carrying a bag that contained a plastic bottle of shampoo, another of conditioner, some lip gloss, a new blow-dryer to replace the one that had disappeared a few days ago — in fact, just after my kid sister Phoebe had packed and left for her summer job as a counsellor at a sleep-away camp — and a pack of gum. The drugstore was equipped with automatic sliding doors that parted as soon as anyone approaching the In door from outside or the Out door from inside got close enough to trip the sensors. I got close enough. The door *swoosh*ed open. In hindsight, I suppose I should have at least looked up before I stepped out onto the sidewalk, but I was rooting around in the bag for the pack of gum, which, naturally, had worked its way to the bottom. If I *had* looked up, even for a second, I might have had a fighting chance.

But I didn't.

My head was down and my attention was focused one hundred percent on the bag and the elusive package of gum when the doors parted. I stepped out onto the sidewalk and *wham!*, something big and hard slammed into me, hurtling me back against the now-closed Out door, which, because it *was* the Out door, was *not* equipped with sensors on the outside and so did *not* automatically slide open again. And that meant that I had no way to escape being flattened by what had just crashed into me, which turned out to be a strong, well-muscled man.

I know. It sounds funny. It's the kind of thing that, if I had seen it instead of been it, I'd have had to fight hard to suppress the laugh that naturally rises in your throat when you see someone slip on a patch of ice and their arms pinwheel and their feet do an ultrasonic shuffle as they try to stay upright. You know you shouldn't laugh. You know it's not nice. But you can't help yourself because, well, it *looks* funny. Looks, but isn't. Right then and there, as all the air was knocked out of my lungs and something that I was pretty sure was the back of my head made a horrible cracking sound, I swore I would never again laugh when I saw someone else go *splat* on the sidewalk.

Then everything went black.

The next thing I was aware of was pain — lots of it. My head hurt, my back hurt, my left leg hurt. Someone said, "Chloe, can you hear me?" The voice sounded vaguely familiar, but I had trouble placing it, probably because of the ringing in my ears. I opened my eyes but was blinded by the sun and quickly closed them again. Someone else said, "You'd better call Bonnie Elliot," which alarmed me. Bonnie Elliot is a doctor. I became even more alarmed when I felt something warm, wet and sticky all over my pants and my legs. My first thought — one that almost sent me into a faint — was *blood*. That's the way it always is in books and movies, right? Someone gets whacked on the head

6

or stabbed or shot and when they finally gather their senses, they feel something warm and sticky. And when they gingerly touch the wet stuff and then look at their fingers, they always see red. Blood.

I reached down with one hand and touched the warm, sticky stuff.

I raised my hand to my face and squinted at it.

The stuff was cream-coloured, not red. It smelled of coconut. It wasn't blood. It was hair conditioner.

Then someone said, "Do you want me to take them down to the police station?"

I opened my eyes again. This time something was shielding me from the sun. I stared up and saw that the something was really some*one* — Ross Jenkins, a friend of mine, even if he is a bit of a choirboy. He looked as alarmed as I felt.

"Geez, Chloe, are you okay?" he said.

If I had been more alert, I might have noticed what was hanging from a strap around his neck. I might have remembered how he was spending his summer. But I wasn't alert. I was fuzzy-headed and confused, and when I tried to sit up, someone pushed me down again.

"What happened?" I said.

"Chief?" someone else said. It was Steve Denby, whose job was to serve and protect the citizens of East Hastings.

"Keep an eye on her for me, Ross, will you?" the first voice said. This time I recognized it: Louis Levesque, my step-father and chief of police in East

Hastings. He was squatting beside me, his hand on my shoulder, holding me down. "Don't let her move. The doctor should be here shortly."

"Yes, sir," Ross said.

Levesque peered down at me. He has a big, bushy moustache that makes it hard sometimes to tell whether he's smiling or frowning, but there was no mistaking the look I saw in his dark eyes. He was worried. And that scared me all over again.

"Hold tight," he said to me, standing up. "I'll be back as soon as I can."

I turned my head to see where he was going and immediately wished I hadn't. A wave of nausea washed over me.

Ross knelt down beside me. "You look terrible," he said.

Good old comforting Ross.

"What happened?" I said.

"Apparently David Mitchell slammed into you."

"David Mitchell? The native activist?"

Ross nodded.

"Why would he slam into me?"

"He was pushed," Ross said. "As far as I can tell, you walked right into a brawl."

"Ross, I was walking *out* of a store."

"Bad timing," Ross said.

"What was the brawl — ?"

I didn't get to finish my question because a pleasant-looking woman with deep laugh lines etched into her face smiled at me and then touched Ross's shoulder, signalling him to move out of the way. Dr. Bonnie Elliot, wearing jeans and a T-shirt, knelt beside me and asked me how I felt and where it hurt. She poked and prodded me, took a long look at the back of my head — "You're going to have a real goose egg there, Chloe." — shone a little light into my eyes and asked me to follow her finger. She helped me sit up and discreetly lifted my shirt so that she could look at my back — "You're going to have a few nasty bruises, Chloe." She asked me some more questions: Where does it hurt, did you lose consciousness, any idea for how long, do you feel dizzy, do you feel nauseous? I told her: everywhere, I think so, no, yes, and not as much as I did a few minutes ago.

I glanced over her shoulder at the swarm of people in the street. Levesque and Steve Denby were in the middle of it. Steve was working the inner edges of the crowd like a sheepdog, driving it where he wanted it to go. He was trying hard to edge people away from Levesque. Most of the spectators shuffled back a little but then stalled, reluctant to give up the chance to hear what Levesque was saying to the two men who were standing on either side of him. One of them was David Mitchell, in black jeans and a short-sleeved plaid shirt, his glossy black hair hanging down over his shoulders. The other man, in blue jeans and a denim shirt open over a white T-shirt, was Trevor Blake, whom I had met once or twice but had never really spoken to. He was smaller and leaner than David Mitchell, but the look in his ice-blue eyes told me it

9

would be a mistake to underestimate him. If David Mitchell was a mastiff, then Trevor Blake was a pit bull.

"He started it," Trevor Blake said, talking to Levesque but looking hard at David Mitchell. "He threatened me. I want to press charges."

Levesque glanced at David Mitchell, who was looking at Trevor Blake with calm, untroubled eyes. "That man assaulted me," he said to Levesque. "I have witnesses."

Levesque looked over at me. Then he turned and said something to Steve Denby. Steve nodded.

"We're going to take this to the station," Levesque said to the two men. Neither of them protested. Levesque led David Mitchell to a squad car that was parked in the middle of the street and put him in the back seat. Trevor Blake went with Steve. Levesque said something to David Mitchell before shutting the door. Then he strode over to where I was standing.

"How is she?" he said to Dr. Elliot.

"Nothing is broken. But I'd like to check her out at the office. Do you want me to call Sheila?" She meant my mother.

Levesque shook his head. "No, I'd better do that. Can you keep her until Sheila picks her up?"

"Uh, hello," I said. "In case anyone's interested, there's nothing wrong with my hearing."

Levesque gave me sharp look, as if he suspected that what had happened had been my fault. I suppose, given my history, that this was understandable. Then his eyes softened a little.

"You okay?" he said.

I nodded. "I was minding my own business," I said. "I didn't say anything or do anything or . . . "

I wasn't one hundred percent sure, on account of that darned moustache, but I think he smiled.

"I know. Go with Bonnie. I'll have your mother pick you up."

He turned away as Dr. Elliot put an arm around me to help me stand up. When I got to my feet, a tidal wave of nausea swept over me and, I couldn't help it, I threw up. All over the sidewalk. In full public view. Levesque turned back, looked at me, looked at the ground and shrugged. What else could he do?

chapter 2

Dr. Elliot drove me back to her office and helped me inside. Before she finished checking me out, my mother arrived, flushed and breathless. She flung her arms around me and hugged me tightly, which, of course, made me yelp in pain, which, of course, scared my mother. She jumped back as if I had just burst into flame. Dr. Elliot had to work hard to reassure her that I was fine.

"She'll have a few bruises," she said. "And she got quite a crack on the head, so you should check on her regularly tonight." When my mother's eyes widened in alarm, Dr. Elliot handed her a print-out on head injuries. "Wake her up every hour. If you have any difficulty or if she seems disoriented, call me." She turned to me. "If you feel dizzy or nauseous or get blurred vision, tell your mother."

My mother held my hand on the way to the car and packed me into the front seat as if I were an invalid. I think she would have buckled my seat belt for me if I hadn't stopped her. When we got home, she installed me on the sofa in the living room — with Shendor, our golden retriever, flopped across my feet — handed me the remote and a cup of tea, and said, "I'll be in the kitchen making supper if you need anything."

Levesque came home while my mother was setting the table. He didn't remove his gun like he does when he's home for the evening. He bent to scratch Shendor behind the ears, which turned the dog to mush. It always does. Apparently no one can scratch ears as well as Levesque can. Then he looked at me and said, "How are you feeling?"

"A little sore, but otherwise okay. What was that all about, anyway?" I had been watching the local news, hoping for a mention of the incident. But the nearest TV station was one hundred kilometres away and, anyway, I didn't remember seeing any TV cameras in the street.

"Supper's ready," my mother said. "Do you want me to bring you a tray, Chloe?"

"No, it's okay. I'll eat with you." I got up off the sofa to prove to her that I was fine. And I was, too, except that I stood up too fast, and the room started to spin. A firm hand grabbed me. Levesque.

"Maybe I should call Bonnie," my mother said, alarmed again.

"Mom, I'm fine. Really." I looked up at Levesque, who was still holding my arm. "Really."

He released me and stepped back. I made it to the kitchen without any trouble, and my mother started to relax when she saw that there was nothing wrong with my appetite. It didn't hurt that she had made one of my favourite meals — chicken Caesar. While we ate, Levesque explained what had happened, which turned out to be a difference of opinion over the construction of a new golf course in East Hastings.

13

"Those two got into a shoving match over *golf?*" I said. "If you ask me, guys take sports way too seriously."

"It wasn't over golf. It was over the golf *course*," Levesque said.

"In that case, put me in the anti-golf-course camp," I said. I had never liked golf. Now I hated it.

"The argument wasn't over whether or not a new golf course should be built," Levesque said. "There's general agreement that it would be a good thing. It would keep the tourists happy, maybe even attract some new ones. And it would create jobs, both building it and staffing it."

"So what's the problem?"

"The problem is where the golf course should be. David Mitchell and the band council are saying that the land that was bought for the purpose should never have been sold. They're saying it's a traditional native burial ground. Mitchell says he's made several attempts to present the band council's case to the consortium that's building the golf course — a company down in Toronto. He says they won't return his calls, won't give him an appointment, won't even let him explain his case." He gave my mother a look that tripped her alarm system. And no wonder. It wasn't the soft-eyed smile that said he was home for the evening and glad of it. It was the exact opposite.

"No," she said.

"No what?" I said.

My mother stood up, shaking her head.

"You *promised,*" she said. "We need to get away. *You* need to get away, especially after . . . " Her voice trailed off. She didn't have to finish her sentence.

I knew what she meant. So did Levesque. She meant, especially after Levesque had been shot, which he had been, a couple of months back. Especially after my mother had been terrified — we all had — that we were going to lose him for good. And especially now that she knew how much she would have lost. "Louis," she said, "I've made all the arrangements."

Levesque set aside his fork and sat back in his chair.

"I'm hoping we can get the situation under control," he said. "I've already spoken to Howard Eckler." Mr. Eckler was mayor of East Hastings. "If worst comes to worst, you can go on ahead to Montreal and I'll meet you there."

Oh-oh.

My mother and Levesque were scheduled to leave for a vacation in a week. They were planning to spend a few days in Montreal visiting my sister Brynn, some of their old friends and Levesque's relatives, before flying to Paris. I had been looking forward to it almost as much as they had — maybe more — because with them gone and Phoebe away at camp, I would have the house to myself — well, except for Shendor — for three glorious weeks.

"But, Louis — "

"That's worst case, *cherie.*"

"But Paris." My mother had been to Paris once,

when she was twenty. She said it was the most beautiful city in the world — and the most romantic. She had been planning this trip for months, even before Levesque had ended up in the hospital. They hadn't taken a honeymoon after they got married. This was supposed to be it.

"We'll get to Paris," Levesque said. "I promise." He got up and wrapped his arms around her. She protested at first, but finally laid her head against his chest and put her arms around his waist. That was my cue to get lost. At least, I thought it was.

"It's a beautiful evening," Levesque said to my mother. "Why don't you go and sit outside. Chloe and I will clean up."

"Hey! I'm supposed to be taking it easy, remember?"

He gave my mother a pat on the bottom to propel her out the door. "I'll bring you a cup of coffee," he called after her.

Right. "You're going back to work as soon as you deliver it, aren't you?" I said.

Instead of answering, he fiddled with the coffee maker. I started to rinse dishes, which Mom insisted we do before we put them into the dishwasher. My feeling on the subject: what the heck was the dishwasher for?

"You don't think the fight over the golf course is finished, do you?" I said.

Levesque shrugged. "They're scheduled to break ground on construction in the next day or so," he said. "Mitchell told the crew boss that it would be a

16

bad idea to move in the bulldozers." He measured some coffee into a filter, filled the well with water and flipped the On button. "How would you like to go to Montreal with your mother?"

"No, thanks," I said, bending slowly to load the dishwasher. Hey, wait a minute. Where had that question come from? And why had he said *with your mother* instead of *with us*? He had promised her Paris. I had heard him. I thought back to what he had said. Oh. He had promised her they would get to Paris, but he hadn't promised her *when*. I straightened up and looked at him. "You're not planning to bail on Mom, are you? Because if you are — "

"I'm not sure I want to leave you here alone under the circumstances."

"What circumstances? I'm old enough to look after myself. And someone has to take care of Shendor. Besides, I start my job tomorrow." My summer job was similar to Phoebe's job as a camp counsellor, except that it involved fewer children (only one, in fact); no bug-ridden, so-called rustic cabins; no campfire singalongs; and evenings and weekends off. Oh, and I was going to earn more than Phoebe. "When Mom was making the arrangements, you both thought I'd be fine here alone. As far as I know, nothing's changed."

"From what I've heard, David Mitchell generally means what he says," Levesque said.

"What does that have to do with me?"

"He's done some time off and on over the years,

some of it small stuff like disturbing the peace, some of it more serious — property offences, trespassing, assault, resisting arrest."

"I still don't see what that has to do with me staying here alone."

"He says he's going to stop them from breaking ground on that golf course. I don't think he's going to succeed in the long run — "

In the long run . . .

" — but he's sure going to try. I think everyone can count on that."

Which still didn't answer my question.

"The crew boss," Levesque said, spelling it out for me. "The guy who's in charge of the golf course construction . . . It's Trevor Blake."

That explained why the two of them had been brawling, but it didn't explain why it should matter to me.

"So?" I said.

"So, he's Mrs. Blake's ex-husband."

Mrs. Blake was the woman I was going to be working for starting tomorrow. I'd been hired to look after her ten-year-old daughter Jessie for the summer while Mrs. Blake worked.

"So?" I said again. I still didn't see what he was getting at.

"Apparently the Blakes are on good terms. They have joint custody of their daughter. Trevor Blake makes a point of seeing her almost every day."

That's when I remembered what David Mitchell had said when he had come to my school — how native people had to be prepared to defend their rights by any means necessary.

"You don't think David Mitchell would hurt Jessie, do you?" I said. Or me, for that matter.

"I don't know," he said. "But I don't like the idea of you being anywhere near the line of fire."

"Line of fire?"

"A figure of speech. But I'd feel a lot better if you were out of harm's way."

"I already accepted the job."

"I'm sure Mrs. Blake would have no trouble finding someone else."

"Oh, so you'd feel better if someone *else*'s kid was in the line of fire?"

He stared at me for a moment, a hard, serious look on his face that was impossible to read. Then he took a mug from the cupboard and filled it with coffee.

"I'd appreciate it if you wouldn't mention this conversation to your mother."

"So you're not going to get her to pressure me to quit?"

He added some milk to the mug. "I'm going to see where this goes over the next couple of days." He turned to put the milk into the refrigerator. "And Chloe? If anything happens that makes your mother worry about you being here alone, someone's going to have to change their plans. I'd prefer it if it weren't your mother. You understand?"

I nodded. I understood, all right. But I didn't like it.

chapter 3

How I found out that my picture was on the front page of the *East Hastings Beacon* is this:

When I went downstairs on Monday morning, Levesque was already sitting at the kitchen table, the daily newspaper from Toronto spread out in front of him, a mug of black coffee at hand.

"How are you feeling?" he said.

"I still hurt in a few places."

I didn't say that I was also exhausted thanks to my mother having shaken me awake every hour on the hour all night, and insisting each time that I answer a skill-testing question, such as: "When is my birthday, Chloe?" "When did Louis and I get married, Chloe?" "What was our address back in Montreal?" My answers were intended to reassure her that I hadn't suffered any brain damage. And mostly she was reassured, until I stumbled over her mother's maiden name. When I finally got it, she was so relieved that she gave me a gigantic bear hug. All in all, it had not made for a restful night.

"What time do you get off?" Levesque said.

"Five. Why?"

"I thought we could get in some driving practice later."

The offer should have thrilled me. In a place like East Hastings, which is (a) small and (b) in the middle of nowhere (unless you're a tourist, in which case it's in the middle of *cottage country!*), if you want to get from where you are to pretty much anywhere else and you don't have a driver's licence and access to a car, you have to rely on spotty bus service, rides from friends and relatives, a bicycle — my preferred option now that the weather was warm — or your own two feet. But learning to drive is like learning anything else. A lot depends on the teacher and how you feel about him or her.

"Well, I — "

"Meet me at the police station when you get off. I have a surprise for you."

"Surprise? What kind of surprise?"

The phone rang. Levesque glanced from me to the kitchen telephone that was right at my elbow. I picked up the receiver and said hello, half expecting to hear Steve Denby's voice on the other end of the line.

But it wasn't Steve.

It was a deep-voiced, stern-sounding man who asked to speak to Chief Levesque. I handed Levesque the phone, grabbed my backpack and my bike helmet, and went outside.

The *Beacon* was lying face up on the porch. The photo on the front page — in glorious full colour — was of me, lying on the sidewalk in front of the drugstore, my head half-raised, my eyes half-closed. I looked like someone who had passed out after too much partying. In the background — *way* in the background — I could make out two angry men — David Mitchell and Trevor Blake. The headline read: "Bystander injured in golf course melee." The photo credit read: Ross Jenkins. Was he ever going to be sorry the next time I ran into him. I tossed the paper into the house and went to get my bike out of the garage.

* * *

Jessie Blake and her mother lived on the northwest edge of East Hastings in a two-storey brick house with gingerbread trim; it stood high on a rise at the end of a long driveway. The property was huge, and even from the road I knew that the view from any of its windows was going to be spectacular. You could probably see all of East Hastings in one direction and Elder Bay in the distance in the other direction.

I had just turned into the driveway when the front door opened and a small figure exploded out of the house. Jessie. She ran down the drive toward me. I had met Jessie a few months earlier when a group of East Hastings Regional High students had been volunteered (or, as Eric Moore, one of the group, put it, volun*told*) by Ms Peters, the staff advisor for our school newspaper, to help elementary school students produce their first-ever newspaper. Jessie, who was nine at the time, was one of the two photographers for the project. It turned out she had a real flair for the camera. And, for some reason, she had decided that she really liked me. The next thing I knew, Mrs. Blake had called to ask if I would be interested in a summer job. Apparently it had been Jessie's idea.

Jessie greeted me now, showed me where I could put my bike, and led me up onto the porch and into the house. I noticed that the porch was fitted with a ramp as well as stairs, but Jessie didn't explain why, so I didn't ask. Maybe it had been there when Mrs. Blake bought the house.

Mrs. Blake ran her own business managing dozens of properties in the area. Most of them were vacation homes that city people had bought when their children were little. After the children grew up and moved out, the people didn't come up to East Hastings as often. Rather than let their places sit empty, they rented them out and paid Mrs. Blake to make the arrangements and take care of the details. She worked out of an office in her house, but from May through until Thanksgiving — cottage season — she said she was away from the office more than she was in it. She showed cottages to prospective renters, made sure the places were sparkling clean when vacationers arrived, collected the cheques, took care of any repairs and handled any complaints, and checked that no damage had been done and that nothing was missing when the renters left again. During the off-season, she kept an eye on the properties for her clients. She also managed a few buildings in town year-round, including an apartment complex. It all kept her pretty busy.

"I know it sounds easy," she said while she showed me around the house. "But in my experience, any job that puts you in contact with people is a challenge. You never know who you're going to be dealing with or what special needs they may have."

My mother always said the same thing. As a cashier at Canadian Tire, she came into contact with all kinds of people. Most of them, she said, were nice, but it only took one surly, rude or unreasonable customer to cancel out all the pleasant, polite and reasonable ones.

My job was simple: keep an eye on Jessie while her mother worked. Make her lunch and snacks. Entertain her. Take her and sometimes one or more of her friends on outings to the beach or to the park. Make sure she was safe.

The first morning went smoothly. Jessie and I set up a small tent in the backyard. I made sandwiches and lemonade for lunch, and we ate them in the tent. We made Jell-o and put it in the fridge for later. Then Jessie went to change into her bathing suit and gather her swim things. We were going to walk to the public beach up at the lake. I was waiting for her out on the porch when a car pulled into the driveway. The man behind the wheel looked at a piece of paper in his hand and then up at the house, as if to reassure himself that he was in the right place. Then he got out of the car.

"Is this AEB Property Management?" he called to me.

"Yes, it is," I said. "I'll tell Mrs. Blake you're here."

"Blake?" he said, frowning. "Amanda Blake?"

I nodded and went to get her. She followed me outside, but stopped short on the porch when she saw the man standing in the driveway.

"Derek?" she said, as if she couldn't quite believe it. "Derek Lloyd? Roxie called and said a Mr. Lloyd was on his way out here, but I didn't expect it to be you."

The man looked as surprised as Mrs. Blake.

"Amanda?" he said. He glanced up at the house. Was I seeing things, or did he seem a little nervous? "Don't tell me that Trevor is AEB Property Management?"

Mrs. Blake shook her head. "Trevor has nothing to do with it. *I'm* AEB — Amanda Elizabeth Blake."

Derek Lloyd hadn't moved from beside his car. "And Trevor?"

"Trevor and I are divorced."

"Oh?" Derek Lloyd seemed to relax, but he stayed where he was. "I'm sorry to hear that." But he had a funny way of showing it. He smiled. "I was in the area on business and I stopped in town for a bite to eat. I mentioned to the waitress — "

"Roxie," Mrs. Blake said.

Derek Lloyd nodded. " — that I'd been up in Morrisville, checking out places to rent for the summer. She said it was much nicer down here. She insisted that I talk to Amanda at AEB."

Mrs. Blake laughed. "You'd be surprised how much business Roxie sends my way."

"You should pay her a commission," Derek Lloyd said. "She even made the call for me. Then she gave me this address, and here I am." He beamed at Mrs. Blake. "But I had no idea that you were the Amanda she meant. I didn't even know you lived up here. Gosh, how long has it been?"

"Twelve or thirteen years," Mrs. Blake said. "Can you believe it?"

"What I can't believe is that you don't look a day older than you did the last time I saw you."

"Neither do you, Derek."

He positively glowed at that.

"Why don't you come in and take a look at pictures of what's available," she said. "If you see anything you like, I can show you the property."

Jessie burst out of the house just as her mother was about to take Derek Lloyd inside. She was wearing an extra-large T-shirt over her bathing suit and had a backpack half-slung over one shoulder. She was singing merrily to herself, but clamped her mouth shut when she saw a stranger in the driveway.

"Derek, I'd like you to meet my daughter," Mrs. Blake said. "Jessie, this is Mr. Lloyd, an old friend of mine." She also introduced me.

Jessie tugged at my hand. She was impatient to get to the lake. I hefted my own backpack, in which were two bottles of water, a tube of sunscreen, a book and a towel, and off we went, carrying a couple of air mattresses.

We spent a couple of hours at the beach. I don't know why I'd thought I would have time to read. I didn't. I was either in the water with Jessie or keeping a sharp eye on her as she bobbed around on an air mattress. The beach was crowded with both locals and summer people. Jessie found a few friends and asked if she could play with them. I said sure and then spent an hour tracking her movements, a white-hatted needle in a haystack of bodies, bathing suits and sun hats.

By late afternoon, I'd had as much sun as I could take. All I had to do to get Jessie to roll her damp towel back into her backpack was suggest a snack of juice and Jell-o. We were almost at the house when a car pulled in behind us. Derek Lloyd's car. Mrs. Blake and Derek Lloyd got out.

"We can fill out a rental agreement right now," Mrs. Blake said. "It won't take long. We'll just go into my office — "

She broke off when a van turned into the driveway. She held a hand up to shield her eyes against the sun and peered at the vehicle. At first she didn't seem to recognize the driver. Then a smile flooded across her face.

"Well, this is a day full of surprises," she said.

The van came to a stop and the driver's door opened, but instead of the driver getting out, the whole driver's seat swivelled out and was lowered to the ground. I had never seen anything like it. Then, I'm not sure how, probably triggered by some control that I couldn't see, the side panel slid open and a wheelchair was lowered to the ground. The van's driver, a handsome, sandy-haired man, shifted himself with seeming effortlessness from the driver's seat to the wheelchair. As soon as he had made the transition, the driver's seat rose again and swivelled back into place behind the steering wheel.

"Uncle Fletcher!" Jessie said. She bolted toward the man, threw her arms around him and kissed him on the cheek. Now I understood the reason for the ramp into the house.

He hugged her and then held her out at arm's length and examined her and told her how much she had grown.

"Well, it has been almost a year since you last saw her," Mrs. Blake said. "What are you doing up here, anyway? I thought you were down east shooting lighthouses."

"I was. I finished a couple of days ago. And my assistant was due for a vacation. So, since I had a little time to kill, I thought, Why don't I drop in and visit my favourite niece — who just happens to be the best young photographer in the country."

Jessie beamed at this compliment.

"We saw your spread in *Canadian Geographic*," Mrs. Blake said. "It was stunning, Fletcher. You have such a good eye."

"Oh, I don't know about that. Sometimes I think the secret is quantity, not quality. You know, take a couple of thousand pictures and you're bound to end up with a half dozen that are usable. Thank goodness for digital photography — it's perfect for a Type-A personality like mine. Cost isn't a factor once you have the right equipment. You can upload the images, fool around with them, get them just the way you want them. If you don't like them, you don't have to print them. You can just delete them."

Derek Lloyd shuffled uncomfortably, the way people do when they're listening to someone they know catch up with someone they don't know.

"Well," he said, "I guess I'd better get going."

"I'm sorry. I've completely forgotten my manners," Mrs. Blake said. She introduced Derek and me to Fletcher Blake. Derek Lloyd seemed impressed.

"Fletcher Blake, the photographer?" he said.

Fletcher Blake nodded.

"The *award-winning* photographer," Mrs. Blake said. "*And* my brother-in-law."

"Ex-brother-in-law," Fletcher said.

Mrs. Blake laughed. "*Ex*-brother-in-law and good friend. Derek is an old friend too. He and I went out for a while before I started seeing Trevor."

"Where is Trev, anyway?" Fletcher said. "I stopped by his place, but he wasn't around."

"Trevor lives around here?" Derek Lloyd said. He sounded surprised.

"About a kilometre up the road," Mrs. Blake said. "He likes to stay close to Jessie." She turned to her ex-brother-in-law. "If he's not at the park, then he's probably out at the job site. He's got more work than he can handle these days. He landed a major contract. He's about to break ground on a golf course, complete with clubhouse and swimming pool. It's going to mean a lot for this town — we have to keep the tourists and the cottagers happy, you know." She looked to Derek Lloyd for agreement, but he had turned to look up the road.

"I was just about to invite Derek in for a drink," Mrs. Blake said. "Join us, Fletcher."

Derek Lloyd glanced at his watch. "Look at the time," he said. "I have to check in with the office. I'd better run, Amanda."

"What about the rental agreement?" Mrs. Blake said.

"I should probably think it over."

"But you said you loved the place."

"I do," Derek Lloyd said. "But you should always think things over. That's my policy: Don't do anything rash." He glanced at his watch again. "I'll call you in the morning, Amanda, and let you know my decision."

"Well, all right," Mrs. Blake said. She looked confused as she watched Derek Lloyd climb into his car. A moment later he was heading down the long, sloping driveway.

"He said he loved the place," she said, turning to her ex-brother-in-law.

"Then he'll probably call you tomorrow and say he's going to take it," Fletcher Blake said. "In the meantime, I'd like to take you two out to dinner. I saw a nice little French restaurant on my way through town. Wheelchair accessible." He turned a pair of brilliant blue eyes on Jessie. "Would you like to have dinner with me?" he said.

Jessie nodded eagerly.

"After that," Fletcher Blake said, "maybe I could show you how to work the new equipment I bought you."

"Equipment?" Jessie said.

"You didn't think I'd forgotten your birthday, did you, Jessie? I was in Japan for six weeks. That's where I bought it."

"What is it? What is it?" Jessie said.

"A digital camera. And a photo printer. You just plug your digital camera into it and, presto, you're making prints." He tossed her the key to his van. "Check the front seat. There's a big box and a little box."

"I'll help you with the big box, Jessie," I said.

I carried the larger box into the house for her. When I went back outside, she already had her new camera out of its packaging and was pestering her uncle to show her how to use it.

"I guess I'll be going," I said to Mrs. Blake.

"We'll see you tomorrow, Chloe. Thanks."

I strapped on my backpack and my bike helmet and got onto my bike. As I rode down the drive, Jessie called after me, "I'll take your picture tomorrow, Chloe. With my new camera."

* * *

I spotted Ross almost as soon as I got to town. He was strolling down Centre Street, a camera hanging from a strap around his neck, a canvas bag over his shoulder. As soon as I started toward him he made a sharp turn into the Book Nook. If you ask me, he was trying hard to pretend that he hadn't seen me. I locked up my bike, went inside and found him in front of the magazine rack, his nose in *The New Yorker*. When I tapped him on the shoulder, he said, "It wasn't my fault."

chapter 4

"Oh," I said. "So you're not responsible for that picture of me on the front page of today's *Beacon?*"

"No, I swear. I had nothing to do with it."

"Uh-huh. So I guess someone put *your* name on the photo credit by mistake. And I guess that although you were there with a camera — *that* camera, if I'm not mistaken — and you were taking pictures, including pictures of me, there was someone *else* there from the *Beacon* and it was *that* person who took the picture that ended up on the front page, the photo of the innocent bystander injured in the golf course melee."

"I took the *picture*," Ross said. "But I took a lot of pictures. That's my job. It was Mr. Torelli who decided which one to run."

"And he chose an extremely unflattering one of me looking like I was about to throw up — which, I'd like to point out, he wouldn't have been able to do if you had kept your camera focused on the real story."

"I didn't even mean for him to see that picture. Honest, Chloe. I just took it because — " He shrugged.

"Because *why?*"

He seemed to be having trouble looking me in the eye. "I got there too late for all the excitement. So I tried to make up for it by taking a lot of crowd shots. Mr. Torelli said they weren't dramatic enough. Then he saw the picture of you. He loved it. He said it would make a great metaphor."

"Metaphor?"

"You know, the band council versus the town council — the band council trying to stop progress, the town council all for it — "

"By supporting the golf course, you mean?"

He nodded. "And when the two clash, well, the town — exemplified by you — is the innocent, but injured, bystander."

I rolled my eyes.

"It's not my fault," he said again. "You know what Mr. Torelli is like."

I did. He was exactly like a guy who wished he ran a big-city newspaper where he could cover all kinds of crime and corruption, but instead was stuck in a small town where if you wanted excitement in your newspaper, it was strictly do-it-yourself.

"He wanted drama on the front page. There was nothing I could do. He's the boss. Forgive me?"

I glanced at my watch. It was almost five-thirty.

"I have to meet someone, Ross."

He dogged me, begging me to understand until I said that I did, mainly so that he'd leave me alone. Then he started telling me how, Mr. Torelli aside, working for the *Beacon* was a great summer job, that he was lucky to have landed it, that he was sure it was going to help him when he applied to journalism school, unless, of course, he decided on pre-law . . .

"Sounds like it's one scoop after another," I said. "I read your piece on the new crosswalk in front of the seniors' residence. Journalism doesn't get more exciting than that, huh, Ross?" We were close to the police station now.

"Lives could be saved," he said.

"Pulitzers could be won."

He gave me a sour look. "Remind me how you're spending your summer." *Touché*. When I didn't answer, he said, "Check out the next issue of the *Beacon*. I'm working on an article about the park cleanup mess."

"Isn't that an oxymoron, Ross?"

"Ha-ha. For your information, the mess in the park is a big deal. Everyone's talking about it." *I* wasn't. Nor was anyone I knew personally — well, except for Ross. "They had months to get everything ready for tourist season, but it still looks like a construction site down by the spruce bog. You know those signs they have up all over the park: TAKE nothing but memories; LEAVE nothing but footprints; KILL nothing but time?"

Sure, I knew. You couldn't miss them. They were posted along hiking trails and at picnic areas and lookouts. They were supposed to keep tourists from doing dumb stuff like picking wildflowers and dropping litter.

"Well, someone put a sign up by the bog." He fiddled with his camera and then held it out to me. "Look," he said.

It had a display on it, like a small computer screen. "Digital," I said. "Nice. Yours?"

"I wish," he said. "It belongs to the *Beacon*."

I looked at the image on the screen. It was a photograph of a sign, planted among marker pegs, mounds of sawdust and heaps of scrap wood. The sign read:

Jessamor Construction Company motto:
TAKE your sweet time.
LEAVE a big mess.
KILL everyone's enjoyment.

"Someone's not happy," I said.

"Mr. Torelli says it's probably someone from Friends of the Park. He says if Trevor Blake was smart — "

"What does Trevor Blake have to do with it?"

"Jessamor is his company. Jessamor rebuilt the boardwalk through the bog. Trevor Blake is supposed to have cleaned up the mess. But ever since he got the contract for the golf course — "

Blah, blah, blah. I wasn't paying attention. I'd been distracted by what was coming down the street toward me.

"I gotta go, Ross. I'm late for driving practice."

"*Finally,*" Ross said. "Mobility equals freedom. And freedom is a good thing."

He was right. And, truly, I was eager to get my driver's licence. But, hey, we live in the era of automatic transmissions, power steering and cruise control. We've been in this era for some time now. In my family, we have access to several vehicles:

(a) the patrol car in which Levesque spends a large part of his life, (b) the second-hand SUV that Mom bombs around town in, and (c) Levesque's car, an Impala, almost brand new. Okay, I can understand not being allowed to use the patrol car — who even wanted to? But that left two perfectly acceptable automobiles. And in which of those two was I scheduled to practise? Why, (d) none of the above, of course. Instead, Levesque had prevailed on Steve, who drove a car with standard transmission, to let me practise in his car. Levesque's thinking: "If you're going to learn to drive, you should learn to handle the hardest thing on the road. After that, anything else will be easy in comparison." My response to that little bit of logic: "In that case, are you sure you don't know anyone who can lend me an eighteen-wheeler?"

I watched a pre-modern vehicle — a red-and-rust Chevy Vega — slide up the street toward us. I glanced at Ross, hoping that he was walking away. But he wasn't. He had noticed the decrepit vehicle too, and was smirking at it the way guys do when they have access to a decent car and see some poor fool tooling around in a rust bucket. Ross drove his mother's car when he needed to go anywhere and got to use a *Beacon*-owned van for work. When the Vega got closer, Ross's expression changed from smug to astonished.

"Isn't that your dad?" he said. "Is he working undercover or something?"

"Surprise, Chloe," I muttered.

The driver's door of the rust bucket opened and Levesque heaved his massive frame out from behind the wheel. He nodded at Ross and tossed me the car keys.

Ross patted my shoulder. "Good luck," he whispered.

"Well, what do you think?" Levesque said. He ran a hand over the Vega's pitted hood. "Ed Winslow is letting you use it for driving practice."

Ed Winslow ran what he called a second-hand goods business, but which was, in actual fact, a junkyard littered with the corpses of old cars. He had complained about kids breaking in and vandalizing the place — although I couldn't imagine what damage they could possibly do to the piles of rust that Ed had on offer. Levesque had made a couple of arrests, which put an end to the problem. Apparently, to show his gratitude, Ed had let Levesque borrow one of his cars for my practice driving. Thanks a bunch, Ed.

"Automatic transmission?" I said, even though I already knew the answer.

Levesque shook his head.

"Power steering?" I said.

Another shake.

"Cruise control?" I said. Silly question. This baby looked like it had rolled off the assembly line way before the notion of cruise control had even formed in the brain of some engineering genius. Still . . .

Levesque shook his head again. "Lock up your bike and let's go."

He circled around the car, got in, settled into the front passenger seat and was buckling up by the time I climbed in behind the wheel. I got in and stuck the key into the ignition.

"You're ready," Levesque said. Telling me, not asking me.

I put my left foot on the clutch, my right foot on the brake, and turned the key. Then, holding my breath, I shifted into first and gave it a little gas. I don't know if I was too heavy on the gas pedal or too light on the clutch, but instead of gliding smoothly, the car leapt forward like a spooked rabbit. Levesque's hand flew out and he grasped the dashboard. He didn't say anything.

"Sorry," I mumbled, praying that the car wouldn't stall out. Mercifully, it didn't. I drove down to the next intersection, slowed the car and brought it to a stop.

"Where to?" I asked.

"Let's get out of town. You can practise stopping and starting on hills. It's the one thing that seems to scare people the most about driving a standard transmission. We might as well get it over with." He made it sound about as appealing as major dental surgery. "Take the next left."

The next left came up a lot faster than I expected and, as a result, I took the corner a lot faster than Levesque expected.

"You accelerate *out* of a turn," he said. "Not *into* one."

"Right."

"Slow it down a little."

"*Okay*." Geez.

We were on a gravel road that ran north along the west side of the park, parallel to the main road to Morrisville. Every couple of hundred metres or so, a smaller dirt road ran off one side or the other and in through the trees to a cottage that was by and large invisible from the road. Then, after a while, the snaking driveways stopped and we were in deep woods.

"In another kilometre you'll come to a sharp turn. Take it easy," Levesque said. "A little after that, you'll see a sign for Camp Allendale."

Allendale. It sounded familiar. "Isn't that where they're building the new golf course?"

"That's a little farther up the road. Take the turnoff to Allendale, and you'll come to a nice, steep hill."

If it was steep, how could it possibly be nice?

"You won't run into any other traffic. It's a nice, quiet place to practise."

There was that word again — *nice*.

"Slow down a little."

I slowed. A little. And started to manoeuvre around the turn. Boy, he wasn't kidding. It was so sharp you could have sliced bread on it. Then —

"Brake," Levesque said, just as I was registering the massive tree that lay across the road. "Brake now, Chloe." Later, I was amazed at how calm his voice had sounded. Or maybe it had just sounded calm in comparison to my panic.

40

I braked. I braked so hard I thought my foot would push the brake pedal through the floor of the car. Levesque reached across me and grabbed the wheel and turned it a little so that when the car hit, it wasn't head-on. It didn't hit hard — it made more of a *crunch* than a *bam!* — and then we weren't moving anymore.

"Are you okay?" Levesque said. I nodded, even though I was shaking all over. "Get out of the car, Chloe."

I couldn't move. My hands had somehow become glued to the steering wheel.

Levesque leaned over me and pushed open the driver's-side door.

"Get out of the car, Chloe," he said again, his voice soft and encouraging.

A moment later I was standing on gravel beside the car, but I don't actually remember getting out. Levesque shifted into the driver's seat and got out on the same side as I had.

"You sure you're okay?" he said.

I nodded again, but I was thinking about the movie they had shown us in driver education — a crash-test dummy behind the wheel of a car smashing into a brick wall at a mere forty kilometres an hour. Hello, wall. Goodbye, crash-test dummy. Of course, the dummy hadn't been wearing a seat belt.

Levesque walked to the side of the road and jumped the deep ditch that ran alongside it so that he could inspect the base of the tree. He stood there for a few moments, staring at it, before crossing the ditch again and inspecting the damage done to the car. He dug his cell phone out of his pocket and punched in some numbers.

"Hello, Mort? Louis Levesque. Listen, Mort . . ."

I heard his voice. I heard him telling Mort, whoever he was, roughly where we were. I heard him say to Mort, "Stop by the police station, will you, Steve will give you something to bring with you." Then he called Steve and told him what he wanted.

"I'll eventually need a ride," he said. "I'll call you."

He finished talking to Steve, slipped his phone back into his pocket and peered at me.

"Come here," he said. He led me away from the car and over to a rock outcropping at the side of the road. "Sit down," he said.

"If you hadn't been in the car — "

"If I hadn't been in the car, you wouldn't have been driving. You're not licensed."

"How did that tree get there, anyway?" I said.

"It looks like someone cut it down."

"But why? Who would do something like that?"

"It's a good thing I'm a police officer," Levesque said.

"You mean, so you can find out?"

"I mean, because I took an oath to uphold the law, not to break it, which means that when I find out who did this, I won't be able to do what I feel like doing." He wasn't smiling when he said it.

chapter 5

Mort turned out to be a tow-truck driver. He also turned out to be the kind of guy who you figured must have bribed someone at the licensing bureau because when he climbed down out of the cab of his truck he said, "What seems to be the trouble, Chief?" as if it weren't perfectly obvious.

"I'm going to need a tow back to town," Levesque said, showing far more patience than I would have under the circumstances. "Did you stop by the police station?"

"Sure did," Mort said. But he stood where he was, gazing at the tree that lay across the road.

After a few moments Levesque said, "And?"

"Oh," Mort said. He stared at the tree a little longer, then loped back to the truck, opened the cab door and reached inside. He pulled out a case, which he carried back to Levesque. "You want me to hook her up, Chief?" he said, nodding at the battered Vega.

"In a minute," Levesque said.

Mort went back to his truck. He leaned against it, fished a pack of cigarettes from the pocket of his shirt and lit up to watch the proceedings.

Levesque pulled a camera from the case and started taking pictures — of the car, of the tree, of the base of the tree where it had been cut, of the ground around the tree. He took out a roll of crime-scene tape and ran it around a wide perimeter of trees. He had just signalled to Mort that he could hook up the car when I heard another vehicle approaching. Levesque walked quickly down the road and waved his arms to stop an oncoming flatbed truck loaded with what looked like building materials. I saw Levesque call up to the driver. The driver jumped down, and he and Levesque spoke for a few minutes. The driver did not look happy, but he climbed back up into the cab of his truck and began the tricky business of backing down the road again until he could find some place to turn around.

"Who was that?" I said when Levesque came back to where I was sitting. I had stopped shaking, but I still couldn't stop thinking about what a close call we'd had.

"One of the subcontractors working on the golf course," Levesque said. "He's making a delivery to the site."

"You mean, *not* making a delivery. You think that's why the tree was cut down? To stop him?"

Levesque's expression was unreadable.

"We're ready, Chief!" Mort called. He had hooked Ed Winslow's old rust bucket to the tow truck and was ready to go.

"You go with Mort," Levesque said.

"What about you?"

"I need to look around some more. Steve's going to drive out and pick me up."

I glanced at Mort, who was climbing up into the cab of his truck.

"I'll wait with you," I said to Levesque. "Besides, my bike is in town."

He shook his head. "Mort will drop you at the house. I'll pick up your bike later. And Chloe? I'd just as soon no one knew yet that it wasn't an accident. Okay?"

I glanced over at Mort.

"I already cautioned him not to say anything. And when I say no one, I mean no one. Okay?"

"What about Mom?"

His look said it all. And that bothered me because that was the second time in as many days that he had asked me — well, sort of asked me — to keep something from my mother.

I don't know what Levesque told my mother, but he must have called her and told her something because she was waiting at the foot of the driveway when Mort pulled over to let me off.

"Are you okay?" she said after I jumped down from the cab.

"I'm fine."

"Louis said you had an accident." She looked at the smashed-in side of the car. "What happened?"

"It looks worse than it is," I said.

My mother looked at the car again and frowned. "What did you hit?"

"A tree," I said. That, at least, was true. "Do I have time for a shower before supper?"

She nodded.

As I went into the house, she was still standing at the end of the driveway, watching Mort's tow truck haul away the now even more beat-up Vega.

Mrs. Blake called when I got out of the shower. She wanted to know if I could baby-sit Jessie the next night. I said I could. It wasn't as if I had a full social calendar.

Levesque didn't get home until after my mother was in bed. He came out onto the back porch, where I was sitting, reading. He glanced at me on his way to the railing, which he leaned against while he looked up at the stars.

"Did you find out who did it?" I said.

"Not yet."

"This has something to do with the new golf course, doesn't it?"

He kept gazing up at the glitter-strewn sky.

"Right," I said. "It's police business, Chloe. I can't discuss it with you, Chloe. Never mind that I was the one who smashed into it."

He turned slowly and looked evenly at me. "I don't want you to be spooked by what happened. The sooner you get back behind the wheel, the better. We should practise again tomorrow."

"I can't. I'm staying late at Mrs. Blake's. She asked me to baby-sit."

"Well, as soon as possible after that then," he said. Oh joy.

* * *

The next morning, after my mother had left for her pre-work walk with her best friend and my French teacher Jeanne Benoit, while Levesque was enjoying a leisurely second cup of coffee, and while I was rushing around gathering my things so that I wouldn't be late for work, the doorbell rang.

"Get that, will you, Chloe?" Levesque called from the kitchen.

Right.

I opened the front door, keeping a firm grip on Shendor, the family greeter. David Mitchell was standing on our front porch, holding something in a paper bag.

"I think I owe you an apology," he said.

"For nearly causing a head-on collision yesterday?" I said. And, okay, maybe it was a slight exaggeration, but my near-crash had kept me awake half the night. I kept imagining what would have happened if Levesque had been staring out the window or if he had been dozing. I tried to tell myself that he would never have done either of those things while he was supposed to be giving me a driving lesson. But the thought nagged at me: accidents — serious accidents — happen precisely when people are doing what they aren't supposed to be doing. "I know you want to stop the golf course," I said. "And I know you believe in using any means necessary. But I could have been seriously hurt — and I have nothing to do with the golf course."

David Mitchell peered into my eyes. "The apology is for what happened in front of the drugstore," he said. "I brought you a peace offering." He extended the bag to me. I wanted to refuse it. I wanted to tell him that no peace offering could make up for the scare I'd had yesterday. But he was staring at me so intently as he held out the bag that I couldn't do it. I took it from him and opened it. There was a book inside — a history of Canada's Aboriginal peoples. "I thought you'd find it interesting," David Mitchell said. Then his eyes shifted upward, and I became aware that someone was standing behind me. "Chief," he said, his tone cooler now.

"Mr. Mitchell," Levesque said.

"I was just apologizing to your daughter."

"For?"

"For what happened in front of the drugstore the other day." He looked at me again. "I hope you weren't badly hurt."

I didn't answer.

"And," he said, shifting back to Levesque, "I heard you were looking for me — something about that tree on the road out near Allendale."

"Are you responsible for that?" Levesque said. He'd come out of the house and was standing beside me now.

"Why are you asking me?" David Mitchell said. "A lot of people are upset about this golf course business."

"Did one of your people cut down that tree?" Levesque said.

"Something happens and you assume we're responsible. Have you considered the possibility that one of Bryce Fuller's own men did it, to make us look bad?"

Levesque didn't answer.

"I'm sorry about what happened to your daughter," David Mitchell said, looking at me again. "Both times." He turned to Levesque. "This golf course business could get ugly."

"It better not," Levesque said.

"Well, I guess that's up to Bryce Fuller, because we're not backing down."

They stared at each other for a few moments, two big, stubborn men, sizing each other up. Then David Mitchell walked down off the porch.

"Who's Bryce Fuller?" I said. Levesque didn't answer. He was watching David Mitchell get into an old grey van. "I said, who's Br— "

"You're going to be late," Levesque said.

I glanced at my watch. Geez! I dashed to grab my bike helmet and backpack.

* * *

Jessie was out in front of her house, posing her friend Megan and happily taking her picture with the new camera her uncle had bought her.

"Chloe," she called. "Come on. I want to take your picture."

"Give me a minute, Jessie. I want to let your mother know I'm here."

I propped my bike against the porch and knocked on the door. Mrs. Blake had a cell phone in her hand when she answered. She let me in, said, "One sec," and put the phone to her ear.

"Me too, Derek," she said. "I know you would have liked it here." I guessed Mr. Lloyd had decided against taking the place that Mrs. Blake had showed him. "Yes. Maybe next year."

She sighed as she folded the phone and slipped it into her purse. "I have to run up to the lake," she said. "One of my clients has managed to lock himself and his whole family out of their cottage — and the family dog inside. The dog is a puppy. A very badly trained puppy. In a fully furnished luxury cottage." She rolled her eyes. "I have to deliver the spare key and do a quick check for damage."

After Mrs. Blake left, I herded Jessie and Megan into the backyard, where Jessie took what seemed like dozens of pictures.

After lunch, we walked up the road to the lake where the two girls swam and floated on air mattresses while I kept an eye on them. That's what I was doing when a shadow fell across my legs and didn't move away. I looked up at a tall, lean, tanned and droolingly good-looking guy in a surfer-style bathing suit.

"Hi," he said and, boy, his smile could have lit up the whole town.

I gazed up at him. I didn't recognize him from school, so unless he had just moved to East Hastings, he wasn't a local. That meant he was either a tourist or a cottager.

"Chloe! Chloe, look at me!" Jessie called from the water's edge. I raised a hand to shield my eyes from the sun and saw that Megan had buried Jessie in sand until all that was visible was a large bump and her golden-haired head. Megan was taking a picture of her.

"Kid sister?" the good-looking guy said.

I shook my head. "Baby-sitting."

A small boy who couldn't have been more than three or four years old charged at the good-looking guy's tanned legs, almost knocking him over. The guy laughed as he bent and scooped up the little boy. "Hey, B.J., take it easy."

"Little brother?" I said.

He nodded. "I'm Adam."

"Chloe," I said.

"So I heard," he said, nodding toward Jessie and Megan. "You up here for the summer?"

"I wish. I'm a lifer. Well, I am now. We moved here from Montreal."

"In that case, you're exactly the person I'm looking for."

"I am?"

"You bet. I'm here for the summer. With my dad and his wife — B.J.'s mother." I noticed he said *B.J.'s mother*, not *my step-mother*. I wondered what that meant. "As a lifer, you can tell me what people do for excitement around here."

I glanced around at the cream-coloured stretch of beach, the clear blue lake and the green forest stretching off into the distance.

"You're pretty much looking at it," I said. "Plus there's a movie theatre in town. And activities in the park most nights — campfires, singalongs, star talks, that kind of thing." I would have needed an electron microscope to detect any excitement in his eyes. "There are a couple of pool tables down at Ralph's. Oh, and there's miniature golf."

"Pool tables, huh? You play?"

How to answer? I *had* played. I wasn't terrible at it, but I didn't play often enough to be good either.

"How about it?" Adam said. "You and me — at Ralph's."

"I work until five."

"Then let's make it after five."

"I'm working late today. I promised Jessie's mom I'd baby-sit." I smiled apologetically.

"How about tomorrow night?" he said. He sank down onto his knees and pressed his palms together. "Come on, Chloe. I'm desperate. If you don't do something to help me, I'm going to die of boredom. What do you say?"

What could I do? I said yes. His whole face glowed from the wattage of his smile. He hung around a little longer and we talked while the little kids played. He was from Toronto. He was going into his final year of high school. He hoped to go to university next year. He wanted to go to school in Montreal where he could learn what he called "authentic Canadian French" while he did a joint major in English and film studies. He asked me a million questions about Montreal. When we finally parted company, I felt as if I had spent the afternoon with an old friend. I floated all the way back to Mrs. Blake's house with Jessie and Megan. I kept thinking about what he had said before he'd scooped up B.J. and plopped him onto his shoulders: "I have a feeling this will be a summer I'll never forget."

chapter 6

All of a sudden, there seemed to be no shortage of good-looking males in East Hastings. Adam from the lake. Fletcher Blake. And now this man, tall, with shaggy brown hair and coffee-brown eyes, looking spectacular in a summer suit and carrying a bouquet of pink roses. I recognized him. I'd seen him the day before when he had arrived in a flatbed truck at the scene of my accident out near Allendale. He looked nervously over my shoulder when I opened Mrs. Blake's front door. Then he turned his brown eyes on me.

"You must be Chloe," he said. "Amanda has told me all about you. So has Jessie. I'm Matt Solnicki."

Matt Solnicki was the reason I was baby-sitting. He and Mrs. Blake were going out to dinner. Before I could invite him inside to wait, Jessie barrelled out onto the porch and hurled herself at him.

"Happy birthday, Matt," she said, and presented him with a card that she had made herself. It had a picture of Matt Solnicki on the front. He was making a goofy face.

"Hey," he said. "Where'd you get this?"

"I took it," Jessie said. She grinned mischievously. "When you weren't looking. And I printed it on the new printer Uncle Fletcher gave me."

He laughed, opened it and read what she had printed inside. After he had thanked her, she took him by the hand and dragged him into the house. I followed.

Mrs. Blake came down the stairs, her golden tan highlighted by the deep yellow of the sleeveless dress she was wearing. She laughed when she saw the roses.

"First you insist on taking me out to dinner. Then you buy me flowers. Whose birthday is this anyway, Matt? Yours or mine?"

"Mine," he said. "And your company is the best present I could ever hope for."

She arched an eyebrow. "Oh? Does that mean that Jessie and I should take your gifts back to the store?"

"Mom!" Jessie howled.

Matt Solnicki laughed. "Me turn down a birthday present?" he said. "Never."

Mrs. Blake nodded at Jessie, who raced into the kitchen and returned a moment later with two gift-wrapped boxes, which she handed to Matt.

"Open mine first," she said, pointing to the smaller one.

He did and exclaimed over the pair of utility scissors inside.

"They're special," Jessie said. "They're left-handed."

Matt tried them. "So they are. They're perfect. We lefties have a pretty hard time working regular scissors. Now if they would only make left-handed power tools."

"Besides being a contractor, Matt's a carpenter,"

Mrs. Blake told me. "The best in the area. He built that bookcase for me." She nodded toward the huge built-in bookcase in the living room. Matt smiled at the compliment.

"Open Mom's present," Jessie said.

He ripped open the second package and found a set of fishing lures inside. He must have been an avid fisherman because his eyes watered up when he looked at them. He took Mrs. Blake into his arms to thank her. Then he bent down and planted a kiss on Jessie's cheek.

After Matt Solnicki and Mrs. Blake had left for the evening, Jessie grinned at me.

"I know a secret," she said. "But I can't tell you."

"Well, if it's a secret — "

"Matt told me. He made me promise not to tell anyone."

"Then you shouldn't tell."

"But I can tell you tomorrow," she said. "He said it won't be a secret tomorrow."

She caught my hand and dragged me up to her room. "Look," she said. Her new camera was on her desk, connected by a cable to what I at first thought was some kind of computer, but that Jessie told me was a digital photo printer. "It's part of my present from Uncle Fletcher. He has one just like it."

He had obviously showed her how to use it because she printed out a picture of me that she had taken the day before. It was pretty good. I asked her where she had learned so much about photography, but knew the answer before she gave it. "Uncle Fletcher."

After she had printed all of the pictures she wanted, we went downstairs and ate the fried chicken, potato salad and carrot and celery sticks that Mrs. Blake had left for us. When Jessie finally went to bed, I plunked myself down in front of the TV.

I heard a car in the driveway just after midnight and then voices talking softly on the porch for a minute or two before Mrs. Blake came inside. She smiled at me, but her smile seemed strained.

"Matt will drive you home," she said.

He didn't seem nearly as cheerful as he had been when he had picked up Mrs. Blake. He threw my bike into the trunk, didn't say a word when I got into the car, and remained silent all the way down the long driveway — not that I minded. I've done more than a little baby-sitting. The men who drive me home afterwards tend to have limited experience with teenage girls because, after all, if they had a teenager living in the house, they wouldn't need me to baby-sit. On the way home, these men either (a) make desperate, but not very effective, attempts to engage me in conversation, or (b) maintain a more or less awkward silence.

Matt Solnicki fell into the latter group. He kept his eyes straight ahead for most of the drive, and a good thing too, because the route he took was one that my mother always slowed to a crawl on, if she didn't avoid it altogether. It was called the lookout road, a stretch of dirt and gravel that climbed steeply to a high point that offered a spectacular view of the surrounding area and then fell just as steeply on the other side. The road was sheer rock on one side and sheer drop on the other, and whenever two cars met on it — one going up and the other going down — they almost touched as they inched past each other. Some of the locals — *not* my mother — used the lookout road as a shortcut. I was glad it was dark so that I couldn't see the drop-off on my side of the car. I was also sorry it was dark because the road was unlit. What if Mr. Solnicki got too close to the edge? But he didn't. He zipped briskly up and briskly back down the other side. We were halfway to my house before he said a word. Actually, four words.

"The Big Four-Oh."

I assumed he was referring to his birthday. "A real milestone, huh?" I said. "Congratulations."

He said one more word, but not until he pulled up in front of my house. He said, "Goodnight." I got the distinct impression that his birthday celebration hadn't gone as planned. I wondered if the secret he had told Jessie had anything to do with it.

* * *

"Guess what?" Jessie said the next morning when I was struggling out of my backpack. "Matt proposed to Mom last night. They're getting married and I'm going to have two dads. Megan has two dads. She says — "

"Jessie," Mrs. Blake said, making the name

sound like a warning. "I didn't say I was getting married."

I remembered Matt Solnicki's glum face last night. He may have proposed, but she obviously hadn't said yes.

"But Matt asked you," Jessie said. "And you like him. You told me you did. And if you get married, I can be a bridesmaid." Her eyes brightened. "*And* I can take pictures for you. I can be your photographer."

Mrs. Blake laughed. "You can't be in the wedding party *and* be the photographer."

"See?" Jessie said triumphantly. "I told you. She's getting married."

"We'll see," Mrs. Blake said. She may not have said yes to Mr. Solnicki, but it sounded like she hadn't said no either. She grabbed her purse from the small table in the front hall, kissed Jessie goodbye and said, "I've got to run." I think she was glad have an excuse to avoid answering Jessie. But she didn't get away that easily. Jessie followed her out onto the porch.

"You are going to say yes to Matt, aren't you, Mom? Aren't you?

"I said we'll see."

Jessie let out a whoop and ran back inside. "Mom's getting married!"

"I don't think that's what she said, Jessie."

But Jessie stood firm. "Whenever she says we'll see, it *always* means yes. She's getting married and I'm going to be in the wedding."

* * *

Jessie and I were out in the tent in the backyard later that day, eating sandwiches washed down with pink lemonade, when, *whoosh*, the tent flap was thrust aside. I nearly had a heart attack. Not Jessie, though.

"Daddy!" she shrieked. She launched herself out of the tent and into the arms of the man who had launched David Mitchell at me.

"Hi, Cupcake."

Trevor Blake swung his daughter around before looking at me.

"You're the baby-sitter, right?" he said. He looked closely at me. "Aren't you that girl who was on the front page of the *Beacon* the other day?"

The girl who was on the front page of the *Beacon*. Not: the girl who, thanks to him, had got squashed by David Mitchell. I nodded.

"Did you clean up the spruce bog, Daddy?" Jessie said.

"What?" The question seemed to take him by surprise.

"I saw it in the newspaper," Jessie said. "There was a picture. It said the bog is a mess because of you. That's not true, is it, Daddy?"

Trevor Blake looked annoyed, but his voice was affectionate when he said, "What kind of question is that? The bog is our favourite place, right?" Jessie nodded. "I've been busy, that's all. But don't worry, Cupcake. I'll get it cleaned up as good as new." He turned to me. "Looks like you've got the rest of the day off. I'm taking Jessie off your hands." He swung her around again. "How would you like to go up to Morrisville for the afternoon, Jessie? The amusement park opened on Saturday. Uncle Fletcher is going to meet us. What do you say?"

Jessie yelped with delight.

The amusement park he was referring to wasn't exactly Canada's Wonderland, but it was perfect for kids like Jessie, and it was popular with tourists and cottagers.

"Come on," he said. He took her by the hand and led her away from the tent.

"Excuse me, Mr. Blake?"

He looked at me.

"Mrs. Blake didn't say anything about Jessie going to Morrisville today."

"I beg your pardon?" he said, but there was no hint of begging in his tone.

"I think I should check with Mrs. Blake."

"I'm Jessie's father." His voice was sharp now.

I glanced at Jessie, who was tugging at her father's hand, eager to go to the amusement park. My cell phone was in my backpack, which was in the house. I wished I had it with me now.

"It's just that Mrs. Blake left me in charge of Jessie," I said. Mr. Blake glowered at me. I remembered that David Mitchell had stood a lot taller and looked like he weighed more than Mr. Blake, but that Mr. Blake hadn't had any trouble propelling him clear across the sidewalk at me. "If you could wait here while I call her and check if it's okay for Jessie to go with you . . . "

"Maybe my wife should have checked with *me*," he said, "before she hired *you*."

Wife. Not ex-wife.

"Because I have to tell you," he went on, "I am *not* impressed with the way you're speaking to me. Jessie is *my* daughter." His face looked like a hard, angry mask, set in concrete.

"I know," I said. I tried to stay calm, but I was angry. He hadn't hired me — Mrs. Blake had. She had entrusted Jessie to my care. Besides, I didn't know what kind of arrangement she and Mr. Blake had. What if she came home and had a meltdown because I had let Jessie go off with him without clearing it with her? I shifted my attention to Jessie. "Jessie, don't you think you should let your mother know your plans? Wouldn't she want you to do that?"

Jessie nodded. "She would, Daddy," she said. "I should tell Mom."

Mr. Blake softened. He kissed her on the cheek.

"Okay," he said. "You go and call Mom. I'll wait out front."

I felt his eyes on me as Jessie and I walked up to the house.

"That's okay," Mrs. Blake said when I reached her on her cell phone. "Just ask him when he's going to drop her off, and leave me a note." What a relief. I sure didn't want to be the one to say no to Trevor Blake. "And Chloe? Can you baby-sit again tomorrow night?" I said I could.

Jessie said, "All right!" when I told her what her mother had said. I made her take a sweater, just in case, and followed her outside. Trevor Blake was leaning against a shiny dark blue pickup truck that looked brand new.

"Well? What's the verdict?" he said.

"Mrs. Blake wants to know what time you're bringing her back."

"Tell her around nine. And don't worry," he said, his voice heavy with sarcasm. "Jessie will be safe with me."

He opened the pickup's passenger door for Jessie and then circled around to the driver's side. As he climbed in behind the wheel, I heard Jessie say, "Guess what, Daddy? Guess what happened to Mom last night?"

chapter 7

You know how you always hear people say that you can never find a cop when you need one? Well, there's a corollary to that.

I was walking up Elgin Street, which runs alongside the police station, when someone called my name. I turned and saw Levesque standing beside a small, wiry man in denim overalls. The two of them appeared to be inspecting what was possibly the most decrepit car I had ever seen — even more decrepit than the Vega, *after* the accident. But that figured, because the man Levesque was standing beside was Ed Winslow.

"Chloe, come here!" Levesque said.

I sighed and headed across the parking lot to where they were standing.

"You remember Ed Winslow?"

I did and stuck out a hand. Ed Winslow wiped a greasy palm on the side of his overalls, to no discernible effect, and shook my hand.

"Ed has another car for you," Levesque said.

The car in question was ten percent sky blue and ninety percent greyish-white primer. I peeked into the ragged interior. Definitely standard transmission and just as definitely no chance of power steering.

"Don't worry, young lady," Ed said. "You know what they say — lightning doesn't strike twice. I know you're going to be good to this baby." He patted the hood of the . . . whatever kind of car it was. "If you could drop me back at the yard, I'd appreciate it, Chief."

Levesque started to suggest that I drive, but — mercifully — was interrupted by the ring of his cell phone. He excused himself and stepped away from us. When he'd finished his call, he said, "I'm afraid we'll have to do this another time."

Whew!

"I'll leave the car in the yard for you, Chief," Ed said. "Keys'll be up under the visor. Gate's unlocked every day nine to nine. You just come and get it whenever you need it."

Levesque gave him a stern look. "I don't think that's a good idea, Ed," he said.

Ed Winslow flashed a brown-toothed smile. "Skipper lets me know whenever anyone even thinks about opening that gate," he said. "I took your advice, Chief. I got a dog. Smart as a whip. Nothing gets past Skipper."

Levesque nodded.

I was on my way home when Ross flagged me down. He had a satisfied smirk on his face.

"You keep teasing me about the stories Mr. Torelli assigns me," he said, "so I thought you'd be interested to know that I have something big lined up."

"I thought you were working on the cleanup mess in the park."

"Done," he said. "I'm about to interview a real celebrity."

"A celebrity? In East Hastings?"

He nodded. "Guess who it is."

How hard could it be? Celebrities weren't exactly thick on the ground up here.

"Is it that Hollywood couple?" I said. A few years ago, a major (mostly has-been) movie star and her only-slightly-less-major (and not quite so has-been) movie star husband had built a so-called cottage on one of the more popular lakes in the area. The cottage was more Beverly Hills mansion than rustic abode — it was, as the media never tired of saying, "eye-popping." Since then the favourite activities of the Hollywood couple, when they were in residence, were sunbathing on the dock (she in an itsy-bitsy bikini) and complaining that celebrity-worshippers kept invading their privacy by cruising their boats too close to *their* water line.

"Boy, landing an interview with either one of them would be a real scoop," I said. "How did you do it? I thought they refused to talk to the local press." That's what had been reported by the non-local press after the *Beacon* had run an editorial that said, basically, that people who crave privacy ought not to build splashy summer houses in plain view on well-used lakes in a densely populated part of cottage country.

"It's not the movie stars," Ross said, a little deflated. "It's a famous photographer."

Famous photographer? "You mean Fletcher Blake?"

He perked up. "You've heard of him?"

"I've met him. He's Mrs. Blake's ex-brother-in-law."

"Well, I saw him in town and recognized him right away. I asked him for an interview and he said yes, just like that. He seems really nice. And he's pretty amazing, when you think about it. Not only is he one of the best-known photographers in the country, but he's in a wheelchair. Has been since he was in his early twenties, but he's never let it stop him. He's done shoots all over the world. He has an assistant who helps him with his equipment. But, still, you have to admire someone like Fletcher Blake, someone who doesn't seem to know the meaning of the word *can't*. I'm doing the interview tomorrow."

I congratulated Ross. Then I went home, had something to eat, showered, changed and headed back into town to meet Adam, who was waiting for me outside of Ralph's, looking terrific in black jeans and a dark green T-shirt that highlighted his eyes. I stared into them and marvelled that I hadn't noticed their colour before — a rich, deep shade of green. He smiled at me and we went inside to shoot some pool. After that, we wandered down to Svensons and got ice cream cones, which we ate while we walked up to the lake and strolled along the beach. Then, even though I told him he didn't have to, he walked me home. When he said, "Do you have any plans for tomorrow night?" I regretted that I had agreed to baby-sit again for Mrs. Blake. I regretted it even more the next night.

* * *

Jessie was in bed and I was dozing off when Mrs. Blake and Matt Solnicki got home, around midnight. Mr. Solnicki said he'd drive me home. Just like the last time, he put my bike in the trunk and took the lookout road. And just like the last time, he was silent. By the time we had reached the lookout, he still hadn't said a word. I wondered whether Mrs. Blake had given him an answer to his proposal yet, and glanced at him to see if I could tell by the expression on his face. He did not look happy. We had just started down the other side when he finally spoke. He squinted into the rearview mirror and said, "Do you see something back there?"

"What?"

"Behind us. Do you see something?"

I turned and looked out the rear window.

"No," I said, puzzled by the question. Then, "Wait a minute. Is that a car?" Where had it come from? "It doesn't have its lights on. Not even running lights."

Mr. Solnicki's frown deepened. Then — *boom!* — something hit the back of the car and we lurched forward. Mr. Solnicki gripped the steering wheel with both hands.

Boom! The car was struck again, and again we lurched.

Boom!

Boom!

"What's happening?" I said. I already knew, but I couldn't believe it. We were being rammed.

Mr. Solnicki said nothing. We sped forward. I

think he was trying to get away from the car behind us. His mouth was set in a grim expression, and that scared me. I twisted around in my seat to try to get a look at whoever was ramming us.

Boom!

This time we lurched sideways. The other car must have hit us from the side. This time I screamed.

"Hold on," Mr. Solnicki said. He must have pushed the gas pedal to the floor because we were racing now. I glanced out the window, but all I could see was darkness.

Boom!

Boom!

Mr. Solnicki swore.

Boom!

Then everything turned upside down.

chapter 8

I heard screaming — loud, hysterical, non-stop. I think it was me, shrieking with terror as we flew off the road and then, after more screaming, hit the ground below with a bang and rolled over. Everything went quiet.

It took a while — maybe seconds, maybe minutes, maybe longer — before I realized that the car had settled on its side, which was why I was hanging at a funny angle, half-cradled by an airbag. I turned my head to look down at Mr. Solnicki. He was resting against the driver's-side airbag. He wasn't moving.

I struggled against gravity to open the passenger door. It took a while. It was heavy and I had to push straight up to get it to open. Then I had to hold tight as I worked to release my seat belt and not fall down onto Mr. Solnicki. I was shaking all over as I slowly dragged myself out of the car.

I stood there for a moment, looking up. We had cleared the steepest part of the road by the time we had gone over the edge, so the drop hadn't been as long as it would have been even seconds earlier. Still, we were down here and the road was up there. I stared up at the gap in the guardrail. My legs wobbled uncontrollably. Then I collapsed and lay shaking on the ground.

I don't know how long it was until I remembered my cell phone, or how long it was after that before I got up and struggled to retrieve my backpack from the interior of the car. Mr. Solnicki still wasn't moving.

My fingers shook so hard that it took me several attempts before I punched in the numbers correctly. When Levesque answered, I said, "There's been an accident."

* * *

I sat, dazed, beside the car for what seemed like forever. Levesque told me it took less than twenty minutes for him to find us. It took longer for the ambulance to arrive and to get Mr. Solnicki out of the car. Bonnie Elliot showed up — I'm not sure when. She looked me over and told me I was lucky that nothing was broken. But she insisted that I go to the hospital in Morrisville for a complete examination. It turned out that I was fine, except for a few bruises and minor scrapes, mostly from the airbag. The doctor who examined me called it a miracle. Mr. Solnicki was less fine — he had a concussion, a broken nose and massive bruises all over his body — but he was going to be okay.

It was four in the morning by the time we got home. I drove back with Mom in her car (she'd driven up to Morrisville to meet us at the hospital). Levesque followed in his patrol car. My mother was silent all the way home. It wasn't until I was in bed that I heard her say anything. What she said was, "Chloe's coming with us."

"I don't think Chloe was the target," Levesque said.

"Two so-called accidents in less than one week?" my mother said. "Not counting what happened outside the drugstore. This is all about the golf course, isn't it?"

"We don't know that yet," Levesque said.

"She could have been killed," my mother said. Then I heard sobbing, followed by the low rumble of Levesque's soothing voice.

* * *

The phone rang off the hook first thing in the morning — my mother's friends calling to see if I was okay, Ross checking on me, a few surprise calls from kids I knew from school but whom I had never really considered close friends. And Mrs. Blake, her voice shaky, asking how I was and saying she would understand if I didn't want to work for her again until the excitement over the golf course was over.

I told her I was fine. I didn't tell her that I had barely slept all night, and that when I had, I had relived that long fall and the crushing impact. I said I would like to keep working for her. When I said that, my mother started shaking her head.

Mrs. Blake said that Jessie was spending the morning with her father and her uncle while she went up to Morrisville to see Mr. Solnicki. But, she said, Jessie had heard about the accident and had been asking about me. She wanted to see me. Did I think I could spend some time with her in the afternoon? I said I could and we agreed on a time while my mother continued to shake her head. After I hung up, she said, "You should be resting today."

"I'd rather be doing something, Mom."

"But you were hurt."

"I'm fine." Well, maybe I was a little rattled. But if I told my mother that, she would probably forbid me to go back to Mrs. Blake's *and* she would insist I go with her when she and Levesque left town.

"Trevor Blake and Matt Solnicki are both working on the golf course," she said. "I don't think it's a good idea for you to be around them."

"I'm not around them. I'm with Jessie and Mrs. Blake — and neither of them is involved."

Tears welled up in my mother's eyes. I hugged her and told her not to worry.

"I won't drive home with Mr. Solnicki ever again. I promise," I said.

Finally my mother relented. My bike had been in the trunk of Matt Solnicki's car when we went off the road, so I borrowed Phoebe's — I figured it was a fair trade for the blow-dryer she had borrowed from me — and rode over to Mrs. Blake's after lunch. Trevor Blake was dropping Jessie off when I arrived. Jessie rushed over to me and asked me a hundred questions about what had happened. Trevor Blake nodded a curt greeting before getting into his truck and driving away.

After Jessie had inspected my scrapes and bruises, we decided to make fudge brownies with thick, gooey icing. Then I left a note to tell Mrs. Blake that we were going to the lake. We found Adam on the beach, building a sand fort with B.J. We joined them and Jessie took pictures that B.J. was only too thrilled to pose for.

"I heard what happened," Adam said. "Are you okay?" I said I was. "It never would have happened," he said, "if you'd gone out with me instead."

We horsed around in the water until Adam and B.J. had to leave. Then Jessie and I headed back to her house and retreated into the backyard tent with strawberries, lemonade and some magazines. We sprawled on our stomachs and Jessie flipped through the magazines, telling me which actors and singers she liked and which ones she didn't. I was paying attention. At least, I thought I was. But it had been a long afternoon after an even longer, sleepless night, and it was nice and cool in the tent. I must have drifted off because the next thing I knew, I heard voices. I opened my eyes and looked around, disoriented. Jessie was still lying on her stomach, peeking out under the flap of the tent.

"Jess— "

"*Shhh!*" she said, turning to me. "I want to hear what they're saying."

"What who — "

"*Shhh!*"

I heard Mrs. Blake's voice. "He waited until this morning to call me. He said he didn't want to alarm me in the middle of the night."

"But he is going to be all right?" another voice said. Fletcher Blake.

"He was incredibly lucky. He could have been killed. They both could have been. Instead, Chloe walked away with barely a scratch and Matt has a broken nose and is black and blue all over. They kept him in hospital overnight for observation, but he's home now."

I wriggled over beside Jessie and peeked out. Mrs. Blake was sitting on a patio chair. Her former brother-in-law sat beside her in his wheelchair, a camera on his lap. I remembered the note I had left on the fridge but hadn't removed when we got back. Mrs. Blake probably thought that Jessie and I were still at the lake.

"Matt asked me to marry him," Mrs. Blake said.

"He did?" Fletcher Blake sounded surprised. I glanced at Jessie. She had told her father two days ago that Mr. Solnicki had proposed to her mother. That same day she and her father had spent the afternoon with her uncle. But it sounded as if no one had mentioned the proposal to him. "Did you accept?"

"Jessie," I whispered. "I think we should — "

"I want to hear," Jessie said in a whisper.

There was a long pause. Then Fletcher Blake said, "Amanda? What's wrong?"

"I haven't given him an answer yet." I heard a heavy sigh. "Jessie would be thrilled to have two fathers."

Jessie turned to beam at me.

"But?"

"If I tell you, you'll laugh."

He laughed right then, a big fake-sounding laugh. "There, I've got it out of the way. Now, what's the matter, Amanda?"

Another long pause.

"I have bad luck with men," she said finally.

"I wouldn't call one divorce *such* bad luck. Besides, it worked out amicably. Trevor is a devoted father. I'm sure he wishes you nothing but happiness."

"I know he does. But that's not what I mean. What I mean is, the men I get involved with always seem to have bad luck. All of them. It's as if being involved with me jinxes them."

"Jinxes them? You mean like me?"

Jessie turned to me, her mouth a little O of surprise.

"You and I weren't involved in the way I mean, Fletcher."

"If we weren't, it wasn't because I wasn't interested. But when you have a big brother like Trevor to compete with — "

"That came after, and you know it."

"After my accident, you mean?" Did I hear bitterness in his voice?

"It wasn't like that at all, Fletcher."

His voice softened when he said, "I know. So what's stopping you from saying yes to Matt?"

That was enough. I was embarrassed to be listening.

"Time to wake up, Jessie," I said in a loud voice. "Your mother will be home soon."

Jessie stuck out her tongue at me, but she played along.

"Oh, that was such a good nap," she said, also in a loud voice. Then she tumbled out of the tent and ran across the grass to her mother and her uncle. She was clamouring for her uncle's camera by the time I exited the tent, stretching elaborately so that they would think I had been sleeping, not eavesdropping.

"Did you take any pictures today, Uncle Fletcher?" Jessie said, snatching the camera off his lap. "Can I look? I'll show you the pictures I took."

"Why don't you see Chloe off first?" Mrs. Blake suggested.

Jessie grinned at me. She had her uncle's camera in her hand and was looking at the display screen as we walked to the front of the house where Phoebe's bike was.

"Hey, Jessie?" I said. "How come you didn't tell your uncle that Mr. Solnicki proposed to your mother? You told your dad, didn't you?"

Jessie nodded but didn't look up from the camera. "Daddy said I shouldn't tell anyone else. He said it was up to Mom who she told and when. Hey, look at this one, Chloe!" She held the camera out so I could see the screen. Fletcher Blake had taken a series of flattering pictures of his ex-sister-in-law.

* * *

I was at the corner of Centre and Dundas Streets when I saw Mort's tow truck slide by. Hooked to the back of it was a car I recognized. I was pretty sure that the scars and dents on the driver's side hadn't been there the last time I had seen it. The tow truck made a right on Dundas and another right on Elgin, and turned into the parking lot behind the police station. Curious, I followed it and watched as Mort backed the wreck into the police parking lot while Levesque looked on. Steve Denby was standing near the rear entrance to the police station. I strolled over to join him.

"What happened to that car?" I said.

"You mean you don't recognize it?"

"Sure I do. That's the car Ed Winslow said I could borrow anytime I want to do some practice driving."

"Apart from that, do you recognize it?"

"Why? Should I?"

"We're pretty sure that's the car that forced you and Matt Solnicki off the road last night."

I took a step in Levesque's direction, but Steve caught my arm.

"My advice is to keep clear," he said. "The chief's in a killer mood. He doesn't like it when there are bad guys running around. He likes it even less when the bad guys start hitting close to home."

I looked at the grim expression on Levesque's face and decided to wait until he'd had a chance to examine the car and, maybe, to improve his mood.

chapter 9

"Come on," Ross said. "Tell me."

"Is that why you offered to buy me coffee?" I said.

Ross had spotted the wrecked car in the police parking lot too. He had approached Levesque — "I'm on assignment, sir," — and asked him about it, but had been rebuffed with a firm "No comment." Then he had seen me talking to Steve and had wandered over to ask if he could buy me a cup of coffee. Now we were sitting in a booth in Stella's Great Home Cooking, a restaurant on Centre Street that serves truly great home-style food — if what is served at your home happens to be old-fashioned stick-to-your-ribs dishes like roast chicken, Salisbury steak and smothered pork chops rather than, say, Chinese dumplings, *pad thai* or lamb *vindaloo*.

"I bought you coffee because you're my friend," Ross said. "And because I care about you, so naturally I want to know. Was that the car?"

"You mean, the car from last night?" I shrugged. "I don't know. It was too dark."

"But if it rammed the car you were in, you must have seen something."

I shook my head again. Levesque had warned me not to divulge any details. Reason: ongoing police investigation. "So, how did your interview with Fletcher Blake go?"

Ross wasn't that easily deflected.

"Chloe, you were there. You were *in* the car."

"Did Fletcher Blake answer all your questions? Did you find out how he ended up in that wheelchair?"

"Diving accident. Don't change the subject. Tell me about the car."

"Ross, it was too dark."

"But you must have seen *something*. You must have some idea what happened — and why."

"I don't know anything, Ross." Not if you didn't count the few scraps of information that Steve had shared with me: namely, that someone had stolen the car from Ed Winslow's yard (keys conveniently located up behind the driver's-side visor) and had used it to force Matt Solnicki's car off the road, that the car had been found abandoned a couple of kilometres out of town, near where the golf course was supposed to be built, that paint flecks on it appeared to match the paint on Mr. Solnicki's car and vice versa, and that whoever had stolen the car from Ed Winslow's place had also poisoned his dog Skipper before breaking in, to keep the dog from sounding the alarm.

Ross leaned across the table. "Come on, Chloe. Anything you tell me will be strictly off the record."

Right. "This is me you're talking to, Ross. Which means that I've been off the record before and it didn't stop what I said from ending up in the newspaper — "

"You've never been off the record with me," Ross said.

"*And* I didn't doze through Ms Peters's lectures on ethics in journalism. I know as well as you do that there are no hard-and-fast rules about 'off the record,' and that if I say anything that you or Mr. Torelli" — especially Mr. Torelli — "thinks is newsworthy, you'll use it."

"What if I give you my word as a friend that I won't?"

"Is that why you're asking me? Because we're friends?"

He squirmed in his seat. "I won't quote you on anything. I'll use whatever you tell me as background only, as a starting point to get someone else to give me information on the record. Your name won't even come up. I promise."

He looked sincere. And he *was* my friend. Maybe even my best friend — in East Hastings, anyway. I was seriously considering telling him when I noticed that his attention had shifted from me to something that seemed to be happening somewhere behind me.

"What's wrong?" I said.

"That's what I'd like to know." He stood up. I twisted around in the booth and looked toward the front of the restaurant. A crowd had gathered on the sidewalk outside of Stella's. Everyone seemed excited about something — but what?

I followed Ross outside. Ross, intrepid journalist that he is, asked the first person he saw what all the excitement was about, and confirmed the answer by asking two more people. Then he said, "I'd better go." He ran down the street to the *Beacon* office. He was probably hoping that Mr. Torelli would assign him to the story. Who could blame him? It was shaping up to be the biggest thing that had happened in town in a while. According to what people were saying, David Mitchell and a group of his supporters had barricaded the road leading into the site of the new golf course. Now they were defending the barricade. And they were armed.

* * *

I was still standing outside Stella's listening to the buzz and the speculation when a car horn tooted and someone called my name. It was Adam, at the wheel of a sporty little Suzuki SUV.

"Did you hear about all the excitement?" he said. "Come on. Let's go check it out."

I hesitated. Levesque would probably be there. If he saw me . . .

"Don't worry," Adam said. "We'll be careful. We have to be. I've got B.J. with me." He nodded toward the back seat where, sure enough, B.J. was strapped into a child seat. "Hop in," Adam said.

"Maybe just a quick look," I said. "From a safe distance."

"Understood," Adam said. He got out and opened the passenger door for me. My mother would have melted. She loved what she called gentlemanly behaviour.

It turned out that we had no choice but to stay well back from the action, because it turned out that we weren't the only people who had decided to check out what was going on. From where we parked, behind a long line of vehicles pulled over on the shoulder of the gravel road, we couldn't see much. Adam unbuckled B.J., helped him out of the car and hoisted him onto his shoulders. Then he took me by the hand — *he took me by the hand* — and for a few moments, that was the only fact I could register. A really nice guy I had just met, a guy I liked a lot, was holding my hand. We threaded our way through the crowd.

Even with his back to us, Levesque was easy to spot. He was taller than anyone else near him. When we got close enough, I saw that he was standing right at the barricade — sections of tree trunks that had been piled across the road. All of the people on the other side — there were men, women *and* children — looked to be native. Most of them were standing back a few metres. All of them were watching the three men who were at the barricade. One of them was David Mitchell, who was talking to Levesque. The other two stood silently on either side of him. Both were holding hunting rifles.

I spotted Steve Denby. He was trying to disperse the crowd on our side of the barricade. When he saw me, he shook his head. Right. The whole town turns out to see what's going on and he's disappointed in *me*. Levesque would be too, if he saw me.

I was about to suggest to Adam that we leave when a couple of men broke through the crowd in front of Steve. One of them was Trevor Blake. The other was a tall, well-dressed man who said something to Steve.

"Look," B.J. said. His high, clear four-year-old voice cut through the murmur of the crowd. "It's Daddy!"

The well-dressed man turned and searched the crowd. B.J. waved. The man nodded in curt acknowledgement before giving Adam a sharp look. Adam met the man's eyes evenly.

"That's your father?" I said.

Adam nodded. His father turned back to Steve and continued talking. Whatever he said, it worked, because Steve let him approach Levesque. Trevor Blake was right behind him.

"What's he doing here?" I said.

"Knowing Bryce, he's probably trying to take charge of the situation," Adam said.

Bryce? David Mitchell had mentioned that name to Levesque. "Bryce Fuller?" I said.

"You know who he is, huh?" Adam said. He didn't seem pleased.

"I know he's involved with building the new golf course."

Adam nodded. "His company owns lots of recreation properties. Marinas, video arcades, indoor climbing facilities, golf clubs, putting greens. Bryce F. Fuller. He always says that 'fun' is his middle name."

I looked at Bryce Fuller again. He was talking

earnestly to Levesque. On the other side of the barricade, David Mitchell stood perfectly still, his hands clasped in front of him, listening without expression to what was being said. Levesque shook his head. Bryce Fuller kept talking, gesturing with his hands, making it clear that he wanted the barricade removed — *now*.

I'm not sure what sparked it. Maybe David Mitchell said something. Maybe one of the guys flanking him said something. I was watching Bryce Fuller, so I didn't see it. All I know is that one minute Trevor Blake was standing next to Bryce Fuller and the next minute he was half-over the barricade, his face flushed and twisted as he dove for David Mitchell. He must have caught Levesque off guard because it took a second for Levesque to spin around, grab Trevor Blake and order him back. By then, one of the men with Mitchell had sprung forward. I saw the blur of his fist. I saw Trevor Blake reel backward. I heard a shrill sound — a scream? Where was it coming from? I saw Levesque hold Blake to keep him from falling. Then I heard the shrill scream again and saw a flash of red as someone — someone small — darted into the opening near the barricade. Levesque was still holding onto Blake, but now he was trying to restrain him from lunging over the barricade at the guy who had hit him. Trevor Blake shouted names at the man, and the man started forward. Then I saw the source of the scream. Jessie. She had appeared from nowhere and was tugging at her father's arm. David Mitchell laid a hand on the arm of the man beside him, the one who had hit Blake. While Trevor Blake turned to reassure Jessie, the man with David Mitchell said something I couldn't hear. Whatever it was, it got the same reaction as if he'd jabbed Trevor Blake with a sharp stick. Blake wheeled around, oblivious to Jessie's presence now. Levesque had to work even harder to hold him back.

Mrs. Blake pushed her way into the opening near the barricade and wrapped her arms around Jessie. She said something to her ex-husband, but I couldn't tell whether he heard her or not. Mrs. Blake looked around frantically. Her eyes met mine. She and Jessie vanished into the crowd just as we heard it —

Brrrrp, brrrrp.

The bleat of police sirens.

When I turned around, all I saw were backs of heads. Everyone's attention had shifted from the barricade up front to the OPP police cruisers, six in all, that were nosing their way through the crowd from behind. Five of the cruisers stopped about ten metres from the barricade and disgorged ten OPP officers who immediately started pushing spectators back. The sixth car inched forward until it was almost at the barricade. Two OPP officers got out and spoke to Levesque. Levesque nodded at Trevor Blake. One of the OPP officers took him by the arm. When he resisted, the officer said something to him. So did Bryce Fuller. Trevor

Blake let the OPP officer escort him back through the crowd, but not before he yelled something at David Mitchell.

The second OPP officer, who appeared to be taking charge of the situation, spoke to Bryce Fuller, who listened, nodded and stepped back to where the other OPP officers were containing the crowd. Then the OPP officer in charge led Levesque away from the barricade. I caught a glimpse of them, the OPP officer talking, Levesque listening intently, before Adam, B.J. and I were herded back with everyone else.

"Looks like Bryce has finally run up against a situation that he can't finesse by throwing money at it," Adam said. He grinned at me.

"Chloe," a voice said. "Chloe, thank goodness."

It was Mrs. Blake. She had worked her way over to Adam and me. She held Jessie by one wrist. Jessie's camera dangled from one hand. She had a backpack slung over one shoulder and a dazed expression on her face.

"We were on the way home," Mrs. Blake said. "We saw all the cars. We never should have stopped." She glanced back at the barricade. "Chloe, can you do me a favour? Can you take Jessie out of here while I make sure Trevor is okay, and maybe calm him down so he doesn't do anything rash? He has such a quick temper."

"I don't want to go," Jessie said. "I want to see Daddy."

"You can see him later," Mrs. Blake said. She

looked imploringly at me. "Please, Chloe?"

"No problem," Adam said for me. "We were just going to take B.J. to get some ice cream. Then we were going to check out the playground down at the beach. You want to come, Jessie? Hey, you can take a picture of Chloe and me. How about it?"

"Well . . . " Jessie hesitated.

"We'd love you to come, wouldn't we, B.J.?" Adam said.

B.J. nodded eagerly. "Take my picture," he said.

Jessie smiled up at him perched on Adam's shoulders.

"Okay," she said.

Mrs. Blake mouthed a thank you. "I'll pick her up as soon as I can," she said.

"I have my cell phone. Call me if you need to," I told her.

Adam and I shepherded the kids to the car and buckled them in. I tossed Jessie's backpack into the back and we headed into town for ice cream. After that we drove to the playground, where Jessie got so involved in pushing a delighted B.J. on the swings and climbing up on the slide with him, that she seemed to forget about her father. While they played, Adam and I made plans for a hike in East Hastings Provincial Park on Sunday.

Jessie had her camera out and was taking pictures of B.J. when I spotted Fletcher Blake's van at the edge of the beach. He was behind the wheel. He had his camera in his hand — I think he must have been snapping some pictures. When he saw that I'd noticed him, he waved me over.

"Amanda asked me to come and get Jessie," he said.

"Is everything okay?" What I meant was, had his brother been arrested? But I couldn't think of a diplomatic way to ask.

"Let's just say that emotions seem to be running high," he said. "But as far as I know, there hasn't been any violence."

He looked over my shoulder and broke into a smile. I turned and immediately saw why. Jessie was racing across the sand toward us, her camera clutched in her hand.

"Hey, Jessie," Fletcher Blake said. "Your mother asked me to come and get you. How about we take the long way home to your dad's place? I noticed these amazing rock formations. I want to take some pictures. Want to be my assistant?"

Boy, did he know the magic words. Jessie scrambled up into the front passenger seat.

"Did you take any new ones today?" she said as she buckled up.

"As a matter of fact, I did. Of you. Just now."

"Can I see?"

He beamed at her with such pleasure that I suddenly imagined him with children of his own. He seemed to enjoy Jessie's company, and he treated her like a fellow photographer, not a little kid. He handed over his camera. While she checked out the pictures he had taken on the display screen, he turned to me.

"Amanda asked me to thank you," he said. "She said she'll see you Monday."

* * *

When I finally got home, my mother was sitting at the kitchen table, pencil in hand. I peeked over her shoulder.

"Making a list?"

"I should be insisting that you come with us," she said.

"On your honeymoon? No thanks, Mom."

"To Montreal. Away from here. You could stay with Brynn."

"No way."

She stared at me, trying to decide, I think, how hard to push the issue.

"I've asked Jeanne to look in on you," she said.

I thought about how hard *I* should push, and what would happen if I did.

"Okay," I said. "If that's what you want."

"What I *want* is for you to come with us. What I'll settle for is Jeanne checking up on you." She looked like she was going to cry again, so I hugged her.

"Maybe it will all be over in a day or two," I said.

Shendor, who had been lying quietly under the kitchen table, jumped up and rocketed for the front door. A moment later Levesque appeared.

My mother turned to him. "You're home early."

"I can't stay. I just came to pick up something." He continued through the kitchen and down the stairs into the basement, where he had a small office. Shendor dogged him, hoping, probably, that he would say the "walk" word. When Levesque reappeared, he was carrying what looked like a rolled-up map.

"Did you find out who stole Ed Winslow's car?" I said.

He ignored my question and bent to kiss my mother on the cheek. "I'm not sure when I'll be back," he said. He glanced at me. "Didn't I see you out there?"

"Out where?" my mother said. "What's going on?" She had been so focused on her vacation preparations that she hadn't heard about the barricade.

Levesque was looking at me. "Didn't I?" he said, as if there were some doubt in his mind — which, I knew, there wasn't.

I thought about saying, "Everyone else was there," but when an adult — any adult — hears that, the response, without fail, is: "And if everyone else were to jump off a cliff, would you jump too?" It's hard-wired into them.

"Well, I don't want to see you there again. Ever. You got it?"

He didn't leave until I had nodded. My mother watched him go out the door. Then she said, "Out where?" Her smile faded when I filled her in. "Were they armed?" she said.

Why did I have to be the one to tell her?

"Chloe, were they armed?"

"A couple of them were," I said.

My mother looked down at her list again. She didn't say a word.

* * *

Everyone in town was worked up about the barricade. More OPP officers showed up. According to the *Beacon*, not only were they trying to negotiate with David Mitchell and the rest of the protesters to get them to end the blockade, but they were also trying to keep Trevor Blake and his crew from doing anything that would incite violence. At home, my mother was upset because she and Levesque were supposed to leave for Montreal first thing Monday morning and there she was, scurrying around the house, packing and repacking, checking things off her list, doing it all alone while Levesque was out at the barricade, with the OPP on one side and protesters on the other — both sides armed. No one I ran into had anything good to say about David Mitchell. Everyone talked about him as if he were prepared to stay out there all summer, all fall and all winter if that's what it took. I guess that's why I was so surprised to see him where I did.

I helped my mother until she started to drive me crazy. Then I decided to take a hike, literally. In East Hastings Provincial Park. I used to be a real city girl. I used to think nature was window boxes and stunted, smog-choked trees in concrete containers along city streets. I used to think that was as much nature as I needed. Not anymore.

One thing I like about East Hastings is all the space — especially in the park. It's so peaceful and cool in the shade of the maples, elms, birches, poplars, oaks, cedars, firs and spruces. And it smells great — fresh and green and alive.

I decided to check if the spruce bog had been cleaned up. If it had, I would take Adam there tomorrow. I hiked up to the top of a ridge that overlooks the bog — which is pretty much what it sounds like, a boggy, peat-filled wetland brimming with mosses, lichens, even insect-eating plants — all surrounded by a dense spruce forest. It attracts dozens of different kinds of birds, which is one of the reasons it's so popular with tourists. Because the bog is so wet, a boardwalk runs through it. It was supposed to have been rebuilt before tourist season. As I looked down on it now, I could see why so many people in town were upset. The area looked exactly like the picture Ross had showed me — a mini and messy construction site filled with sawdust, ends of wood used in the construction, marker flags on little sticks, and endless metres of bright yellow rope marking off the area. It was hardly nature in its natural state.

In the middle of the mess, using a crowbar to pry down the sign that Ross had photographed, was Trevor Blake. He threw the sign onto a pile of scrap lumber, picked up a clipboard and started writing something. He didn't notice me, which was fine with me. I started to back down the rise. Then I heard something. A truck. It drove up as close as it could and some men jumped out. Trevor Blake said something to them. He waved his arms while he talked, as if he were telling them what to do. Then he handed his clipboard to one of the men and started to walk back to the road. As he did, I turned to leave — and just about jumped out of my skin. Someone was standing right behind me. It was David Mitchell. Tall and silent, he was looking not at me, but down at the road far below. His eyes tracked Trevor Blake as he crossed the narrow blacktop to get into the shiny new pickup on the other side. Only after Trevor Blake had left did David Mitchell turn his dark eyes on me.

"You scared me," I said. "I didn't hear you." I was surprised he was up here instead of out at the barricade. Or maybe not so surprised, considering what he had been doing.

He looked from me back down to the bog. "It's about time they cleaned up the place," he said. He turned to go. I watched him, saw how big he was, and remembered what he had said when he had visited my class, which should have made me keep my mouth shut. But I couldn't.

"Were you driving that car?" I said.

He turned slowly.

"The car that drove Mr. Solnicki off the road," I said. "Was that you?"

He didn't answer.

"Someone cut down that tree to prevent Mr. Solnicki from delivering building material to the golf course site," I said. "Then someone drove him off the road. Was it you?"

Nothing.

"I was in the car with him," I said. "I could have been killed."

"I know. I heard."

"So, was it you?"

A head came bobbing up the slope. Then another. Two men were making their way up to where we were standing — first their heads, then their shoulders and then finally their whole bodies became visible as they climbed.

"David," one of them called. His voice sounded urgent.

David Mitchell raised a hand to signal that he was coming. He turned, looked at me and shook his head. Was that an answer?

"What do you know about me?" he said.

What kind of question was that? "I've heard stuff."

"You've *heard* stuff." He shook his head. "Gerry said you were a smart girl." He meant Mr. Lawry. "Are you sure you're listening to the right people?"

"David!" the man called again.

Before I could ask him what he meant, David Mitchell turned and loped down the hill.

* * *

"But, Mom, he *is* careful," I said over supper that night. It was just the two of us. Levesque wasn't home. My mother was mostly pushing her food around on her plate. I don't think she ate more than a couple of bites.

"He was careful before," she said. "But that didn't stop him from getting shot."

"He's been a cop for nearly twenty years and he's only been shot once. What are the chances it will happen again?"

"What were the chances it would happen in the first place?" She got up and scraped off her plate into the garbage.

"I'll clean up," I said. I don't know if she heard me. She was already out of the kitchen and grabbing Shendor's leash from the hook inside the closet door. As soon as Shendor heard the tinkle of the chain she shot by me and jumped up on my mother, who snapped the leash onto her collar and left the house without a word. I scraped my plate, rinsed it and set it into the dishwasher.

The phone rang while I was cleaning up. It was Mrs. Blake.

"Jessie is missing her backpack," she said. "Have you seen it?"

Her backpack? I tried to remember. She had been wearing it when I'd seen her at the barricade. Of course.

"I think it's still in the back of Adam's car," I said. "I'm sorry. I'll call him now and see if he can bring it over."

"Would you, Chloe? Ordinarily it wouldn't be a big deal, but Jessie and I had gone into town so that she could buy something new to wear. Fletcher is picking us up first thing in the morning and we're driving down to Toronto. Jessie's new outfit is in her backpack and she desperately wants to wear it."

"I'll call him, Mrs. Blake, and I'll get back to you."

I dug out the East Hastings phone book and looked up *Fuller, B*. There was exactly one listing. I dialled the number. A woman answered.

"I'm sorry, he's not here right now," she said when I asked for Adam.

"Do you know when he'll be back?"

"He's up in Morrisville with his little brother. I don't expect them until late."

Great.

"Would you like me to give you his cell phone number?"

I said I would. I called Adam on his cell. He sounded thrilled to hear from me.

"I'm at the amusement park with B.J.," he said. "I promised him we'd go on all the rides and then have ice cream — " I heard the whoop of young voices in the background. "How about if I pick you up a little earlier tomorrow? We can drop off the backpack and then head up to the park."

"I'll have fresh muffins and coffee ready when you get here," I said.

I called Mrs. Blake and told her we'd drop off the backpack bright and early.

"Thank you, Chloe," she said. "I hope it's not too much trouble."

"I should have checked that she had it before I let her go with her uncle," I said. "Tell her not to worry. I'll make sure she has her new outfit on time."

After I finished cleaning up, I put on some music, made muffins, and thought about spending the whole day with Adam. Finally, something to look forward to.

Right.

* * *

Adam's Suzuki pulled into our driveway exactly on time. As soon as I saw it, I raced to the kitchen, poured coffee into two travel mugs, and packed the muffins. Shendor barked and started to paw the door. The doorbell rang a few seconds later. By the time I got to the door with the coffee, my mother was holding Shendor by the collar and chatting with Adam.

I handed the two mugs to him, grabbed my backpack, squeezed by Shendor and told my mother that I'd be back by suppertime. I glanced at Adam when I said it, hoping that the day would go well, hoping that he wouldn't discover by noon that I was boring or stupid or not his type. As it happened, that turned out to be the least of my problems.

We drank our coffee on the way over to Mrs. Blake's.

"Thank you so much for doing this," I said.

"Hey, if it gives us more time together, I'm all for it," he said, smiling at me.

We arrived at Mrs. Blake's at eight o'clock. Jessie ran out to the car to meet us. She was wearing her pyjamas. Adam was getting her backpack out of his car when a van pulled up beside us. Fletcher Blake. The driver's-side door opened and the driver's seat swivelled out and lowered him to the ground. Mrs. Blake came out of the house and waved to him.

"We're almost ready, Fletcher. I just need ten minutes."

"Take your time," he said. He looked tired. But he smiled when Jessie raced over and kissed him on the cheek. "You should go and get dressed," he said.

"I've got a new outfit," she said.

"I'd love to see it."

She grinned and circled the van. I saw her open the passenger door.

"We should get going," I said to Adam.

He nodded. Something trilled. A cell phone. Adam reached into the Suzuki and pulled out his phone. He walked away from me while he listened to whoever was calling.

I glanced over at Jessie. She was coming around the front of the van now, walking slowly as she looked into the display screen of her uncle's camera, checking for new pictures, I guessed.

"Oh!" she exclaimed. "My favourite place."

Fletcher Blake turned to look at her. "Jessie — "

"I want to print this one," she said. "I'll be right back." She galloped up to the house.

"Jessie!" her uncle called.

Jessie was up on the porch now, barrelling through the door. She almost collided with her mother, who was coming out carrying a wicker picnic hamper.

"Hurry up and get changed," Mrs. Blake called after her. She waved at me and thanked me for coming. "I thought we could stop along the way and have a picnic. What do you think, Fletcher?"

Fletcher Blake's face changed when he saw her. He didn't look tired anymore. He smiled and said, in a gentle voice, "You look radiant, Amanda."

She did too, in white summer slacks and a pale blue tank top.

"I can always count on you for a compliment, Fletcher," she said. She tucked the hamper into the back of the van and called for Jessie.

Adam had finished his phone call and was walking back toward me, his phone folded in his hand.

"Jessie! Hurry up!" Mrs. Blake called. She waited for a few moments and then started back to the house.

Just then Jessie ran back outside in her new outfit, her uncle's camera in one hand.

"Uncle Fletcher took some more pictures," she said. "Some really good ones. I printed one out." She handed the camera back to her uncle.

Adam and I got into his car.

"Is everything okay?" I asked.

"That was Alison," he said. "B.J.'s mom. She's mad because B.J. had a stomachache last night. Naturally, it's *my* fault."

"Is he okay?"

"He's fine. He's always fine. She just likes to get on my case."

Oh.

"You know what?" he said. "I don't want to talk about her. I don't even want to think about her. Let's just have a great day."

It sounded like a plan to me. We drove to the park, left the Suzuki in one of the parking lots and, at Adam's request, headed for one of the longer, more challenging hiking trails. It would take us to some of the more spectacular spots in the park, including the spruce bog. After that, we planned to head to the lake and rent a canoe.

"Wow," Adam said a few moments later, for maybe the twelfth time. "I wish I'd brought my camera. This is amazing."

"If you think it's amazing now, you should see it in October," I said. In autumn, the leaves of all the deciduous trees turned every imaginable shade of gold, yellow, orange, red and brown, which contrasted sharply with the deep greens of the firs, pines and cedars. "It's pretty amazing in winter too."

"Except you probably need snowshoes to get anywhere."

"Or cross-country skis."

"I hope Bryce never sees this place. He'd want to find a way to *improve* it."

I laughed. "It doesn't need improving. It's fine as it is."

"You don't know Bryce," Adam said. "If he sees a place that attracts people, his first thought is what he can do to make it attract even *more* people. There was a nice little cross-country place north of Toronto. Very popular. Really beautiful. Bryce bought the place and put up a huge motel, only he calls it a chalet. Now the trails are packed all the time. You have to line up to go cross-country skiing. You feel like you're marching in a parade. How much fun is that? But Bryce is raking in big bucks from it."

I looked at him. "No offence, Adam, but it sounds like you don't exactly approve of your father."

"Approve of him? I can't stand him," he said. "He boasts that his middle initial stands for fun. You should hear what the environmentalists say. They call him Bryce 'F-for-Fast-Buck' Fuller. He's ruined more natural countryside than you can imagine with his golf courses, amusement parks and mountain bike trails. He'd burn down what's left of the rain forest to make a tourist resort if he thought he could make money on it. And he always gets what he wants. Always. Believe me, I wouldn't be up here if my mother hadn't begged me to come."

I waited.

"He divorced my mother to marry Alison, who is, like, twenty years younger than he is. My mom didn't handle it very well. She felt hurt, you know? But she says her problems with him shouldn't affect how I feel and that he's my father and I'll really regret it if I try to cut him out of my life, blah, blah, blah." He scowled at me. "He thinks if he buys me enough stuff, he's being a good dad."

I didn't know what to say, so I didn't say anything.

We hiked along a winding path, climbing steadily until we reached the top of the ridge where I had been standing the day before when David Mitchell had suddenly appeared.

"Okay, now I'm definitely kicking myself for not bringing my camera," Adam said. He gazed out over the expanse of forest below and, beyond that, the black ribbon of road that cut through the park. If it weren't for a dark blue pickup truck parked at the side of the road, we could have had a perfect image of what this part of the country might have looked like before white people moved in and started to trap and log, and then to farm, and, finally, to vacation.

"Hey," Adam said. "What's that?"

"What's what?"

"Down there, near that red stuff," he said, pointing. "It looks like a boardwalk."

I grinned. "That's exactly what it is. The boardwalk through the spruce bog."

"The what?"

"The spruce bog. You know, a wetland. There are lots of different habitats in the park. That's one of them. It's swampy, so the only way you can get a good look at it is from the boardwalk. And that red stuff? That's sheep's laurel." I couldn't help it. I was showing off. "It only grows in this part of the park."

"Sheep's laurel? That's a funny name. Why do they call it that? It can't be because it looks like sheep."

"Actually, it's also known as lambkill. Supposedly it's poisonous to sheep."

He laughed.

"What?" I said.

"It's hard to believe you were ever a city girl."

"Tell me about it."

He turned and looked out over the scene again. "It really is nice, though. Peaceful. And kind of beautiful, you know what I mean?"

I knew exactly what he meant. It *was* beautiful. At least, it was now that Trevor Blake's crew had finally removed the marker poles and flags and bright yellow rope that had kept the bog out of bounds all spring while the boardwalk was being rebuilt. They must have cleaned everything up yesterday, after I had seen Mr. Blake down there with his clipboard. Now the only evidence of their presence was a couple of stray pegs with frayed ends of yellow rope still attached that the cleanup crew must have overlooked. I don't think Adam even noticed them. His eyes were filled with the natural beauty of the place.

"So, shall we?" he said finally.

"Shall we what?"

"Take a closer look at the spruce bog."

We descended carefully along a steep path. Once we got to the bottom, we had to follow another looping trail to the boardwalk, which began not far from the road. I glanced out at the pickup truck that was still parked at the side of the road. It looked familiar.

"How far does it go?" Adam said.

"Huh?"

He was already on the boardwalk. "How long is it?"

"Nearly a kilometre," I said. I ran to catch up with him. He'd gone a few metres, but suddenly stopped and was peering intently into the water. When he turned to look at me, his face was white.

"Adam, what's wrong?"

"There's something down there," he said. He looked around and found a stick floating in the water. He fished it out and used it to poke whatever he was looking at. Then he said, "Oh my god." His knees buckled. His eyes rolled up in his head. If I hadn't rushed to catch him and ease him down to the boardwalk, he would have fallen into the bog.

That's when I looked into the water and saw what Adam had seen. At first I thought someone had thrown an old boot into the water. Then I saw that there was a leg attached to the boot. I picked up the stick that Adam had dropped and gently pushed at the leg until the rest of the body swirled into view — face up and fully submerged. I almost fainted myself.

I took a couple of deep breaths and told myself to stay calm. Then I knelt down beside Adam and touched him. He groaned and opened his eyes slowly. He must have remembered what he had seen because he sat bolt upright, looked into the water again, and threw up. I dug in my backpack for my cell phone and punched in Levesque's number. When he answered I told him what we had found. He asked me where we were, exactly. I told him, exactly. He told me not to touch anything. I said we wouldn't. Then I said, "It's Trevor Blake."

chapter 10

"I'm sorry," Adam said.

"Really, you don't have to apologize." But to be honest, I would have been falling all over myself apologizing if I were in his shoes. Fainting is bad enough, especially for a guy. Throwing up isn't cool, either. But it got worse. When Adam fainted, he lost control of his, um, bodily functions. Well, one of them. And when he'd opened his eyes, he'd been horrified to see a big wet spot on the front of his pants. I suggested — as delicately as possible — that he change into his bathing suit while we waited, but it turned out he wasn't as outdoorsy as he'd seemed at first. He didn't want to change behind a tree. He didn't want to take the chance that anyone would see him, I guess. So he wrapped his beach towel around his waist instead, to hide the wet spot, and apologized to me a couple more times. He wanted to leave. I told him he couldn't because the police — Levesque — would want to ask him some questions.

"But I don't know anything."

"They're still going to ask," I said.

Levesque, Steve Denby and Dr. Bonnie Elliot all arrived at about the same time. Levesque's squad car pulled up about a quarter of a kilometre down the road from where we were. The others pulled up behind him. They walked toward us on the opposite side of the road until they spotted Adam and me near the beginning of the boardwalk.

"What route did you take in?" Levesque called to me.

I told him. He told us to stay put. Then he and Steve examined the road. Steve got a camera out of the trunk of his car and started taking pictures. Levesque looked at the pickup truck. He opened his notebook and wrote something in it. The license number, I think. Then he went back to his car and got inside. I couldn't see what he was doing.

Gradually Levesque and Steve worked their way across the road. After more examining and more picture taking, they headed back the way they had come and approached us from a less direct route. It seemed to take them forever to get close to the body. When they finally did, Levesque and Dr. Elliot stood back while Steve took still more pictures. Levesque asked me to point out the exact route we had taken. Then he said, "Are you okay?"

I said I was fine — as fine as anyone could be under the circumstances. I said that it was Adam who had spotted the body first.

Levesque shifted his attention to Adam. He looked at the towel tied around his waist. He looked at the place on the boardwalk where he had been sick. He was gentle as he asked Adam to describe exactly what he had seen. Then he asked how we had got to the boardwalk and where Adam's car was parked. Finally he said, "You can go now. And, Chloe, go back exactly the way you came, understand? And not a word to anyone about this. I'd like to notify the next of kin first."

Next of kin. Mrs. Blake. And Jessie.

I told him where Mrs. Blake was and gave him her cell phone number. Poor Jessie. She was on what was supposed to be a fun outing in Toronto with her uncle. I pictured Mrs. Blake having to tell her the news. I pictured Jessie having to listen.

Adam started to move as soon as Levesque said we could go, as if he couldn't get out of there fast enough. Levesque laid a hand on his shoulder to stop him.

"Let Chloe lead the way," he said. "Follow her as closely as you can. Okay?"

Adam nodded but didn't meet Levesque's eyes. He followed me without a word. When he spotted his car, he quickened his pace. This time he didn't circle it and open the passenger door for me. He climbed in behind the wheel and started the engine. I had to knock on the window to get him to lower it. He turned to me without really looking at me — I think he was focused on my left ear.

"You can find your own way home, right?" he said. "Because I have to, you know — "

He didn't even try to finish his sentence. He didn't have to. He was embarrassed. And, to be honest, he didn't smell all that great. He probably just wanted to get home, take a shower and climb into some clean clothes. He pressed the button to raise the window.

"Hey, Adam?"

But the window was closed and he refused to meet my eyes.

"Call me later," I said, shouting so that he would hear me. I wasn't sure if I got through to him.

I circled back to the road where Levesque had parked. The two patrol cars were still there — Levesque's and Steve's — but Dr. Elliot's car was gone. I wasn't surprised. It was obvious, even to me, that she could do nothing for Trevor Blake except, as coroner, order a post-mortem examination.

Steve had set up trestles to block off the road in both directions. Now he was busy securing the scene with yellow crime-scene tape. Levesque was standing inside the perimeter, near the pickup truck that I had spotted from the lookout. There were two tool boxes in the truck bed. One was open. Maybe it had been open the whole time, or maybe Levesque or Steve had opened it. The other was closed. So were the truck's doors. Levesque was holding a camera, but he wasn't taking pictures. He was just standing there, looking. Steve glanced at me, but didn't say anything. I perched on the hood of Levesque's patrol car and watched. Levesque sent Steve to the parking lot to check out whose vehicles were there. While Steve did that, Levesque got a video camera out of the trunk of his car and made a video of the scene. Then he went over the whole area step by step. Every now and then I saw him bend down to collect and package something he had found, usually something small.

Finally he went back to the body and — eeew! — dipped into one of Trevor Blake's pockets. He pulled out a key ring and a set of keys. He walked back to the road.

"What are you still doing here?" he said.

"I was thinking about Jessie. It wasn't an accident, was it?"

He looked at me for a moment and then shook his head. "Where's that boy?"

"He left."

"Is he okay?"

"I think he's embarrassed," I said. "He fainted. And he was sick."

"You should go home."

"Do you think it was David Mitchell?" I said.

"Do I think what was David Mitchell?"

"The person who killed Trevor Blake. David Mitchell was here yesterday. I saw him."

Levesque's eyes were hard on me. "What do you mean, here?"

"Up there," I said, pointing to the ridge. "He was watching Trevor Blake."

He asked me exactly when. He asked me how long he had been there. He asked me if Mitchell had said anything.

"So, do you think he did it?" I said.

"Right now, I don't think anything. And even if I did, I wouldn't discuss it with you. Go home."

"I'm staying out of the way. I haven't touched anything."

"Go home, Chloe. Please."

The *please* didn't fool me. He wasn't requesting that I leave. He was ordering me to go. I slid off the hood of the patrol car.

"You and Mom are supposed to leave tomorrow morning," I said.

He looked over my shoulder toward the place on the boardwalk where Trevor Blake's body was now lying. Was he thinking maybe Steve could handle the investigation? Was he thinking what he was going to tell my mother when he finally got home? Or was his mind one hundred percent on business — was he thinking about who had killed Trevor Blake and why? I had no idea.

"If your mother hasn't heard anything by the time you get home, do me a favour," he said. "Don't tell her."

Where had I heard that before?

I glanced at him as I left. He was unlocking the door to Trevor Blake's truck.

A hearse from the local funeral home passed me as I walked back along the road. To collect the body, I thought. Probably to take it down to Toronto. And, of course, Levesque would have to go with it — standard operating procedure in a homicide investigation. If he didn't go himself, he'd have to send Steve. Somehow I couldn't see him doing that.

* * *

I was in the kitchen with my mother, cutting vegetables for a stir-fry, when the news came on the radio: a man identified as Trevor Blake, 38, of East Hastings, had been found dead inside East Hast-

110

ings Provincial Park. Two hikers had found him. The report didn't give the names of the hikers, so I guess Levesque hadn't told the media. Nor did it mention that Trevor Blake had been murdered. In fact, so far, East Hastings Police Chief Louis Levesque was issuing no statements.

My mother set down the piece of ginger she had been holding and looked at me.

Shendor barked and dashed to the front door.

My mother turned and waited.

Levesque was half-crouched when he came into the kitchen, scratching Shendor behind the ears and glad to be doing it, if you ask me, because it meant that he didn't have to look my mother in the eye.

"We were just listening to the news," my mother said.

Levesque gave Shendor a final scratch before he straightened.

"I don't suppose it was accidental, was it, Louis?"

"No, it wasn't."

"Was he shot?" Her face was pale, and I saw her hands trembling at her sides. Levesque must have noticed too, because he caught her hands in his and held them.

"No," he said. "He was found in the water, but Bonnie is pretty sure it was a blow to the head that killed him. We'll know more after the postmortem." He tipped her chin up so that she was looking him in the eyes. "*Cherie*, I just stopped in to tell you that I won't be home for supper."

He *stopped in* to tell her that? Usually he phoned

when he wasn't going to make it for supper. More often than not, he made the call when he was already a half hour or more late.

"Steve doesn't have enough experience to handle this," he said.

My mother stared at him. "Everybody has to start somewhere," she said.

"Things are tense enough around here. I don't want any more trouble." He hesitated. "I have to drive down to Toronto."

She pulled her hands from his.

"They're doing the post-mortem first thing in the morning. I have to be there."

For a moment, she was as cold and silent as if she were carved out of ice. Then she said, "Does this have anything to do with the golf course? Because if it does, can't the OPP handle it?"

"It's too soon to know if it's related. It's my responsibility — "

"They're armed out there, aren't they? That's what everyone is saying. David Mitchell and his men are armed."

"Well — "

"Before we got married, you told me that there was nothing to worry about. You said in homicide, you get there after the shooting has stopped. Then when you wanted to take the job up here, you told me again that there was nothing to worry about. You said it was a nice quiet little resort town. But it's not so nice and quiet. You've already been shot once, Louis. And Chloe has been in two car accidents that weren't really accidents."

"I have to do my job, *cherie.*"

"We're supposed to leave tomorrow morning. We're supposed to drive to Montreal to see our friends and your family. And Brynn. Then we're supposed to get on a plane and fly to Paris — for our honeymoon. And now you're telling me you have to drive down to Toronto in the middle of the night? And I suppose you won't be back until tomorrow night. Is that right?"

He didn't move.

"And then, I suppose, you're going to say that you can't leave because you're the only person who can possibly figure out what happened to Trevor Blake — " She broke off and started to tremble all over again. "He came into the store all the time." She meant the Canadian Tire store where she worked. "He flirted with all of the cashiers. Sometimes he had his little girl with him."

Levesque reached out to put his arms around her, but she stepped back out of his reach, dabbing at her eyes with the hem of her apron.

"You should go on ahead," he said. "I'll meet you in Montreal."

She said nothing.

"If it will make you feel better, take Chloe with you."

"Mom and I have already discussed this," I said. "I have a job, remember?"

My mother remained silent. Levesque looked at her, then at me, then, I guess he couldn't help himself, he looked at his watch.

"Go," my mother said, angry now, although I couldn't tell who she was angrier with — him or herself. "Chloe and I are going to have supper and then *I'm* going to finish packing." When he still didn't move, she said, "Go!" She picked up the piece of ginger and, turning her back to him, began to grate it.

*　*　*

We heard him go upstairs. We heard him open drawers and close them again. I peeked out the kitchen door when he came back downstairs. He was carrying a small overnight bag. He didn't come back into the kitchen and my mother didn't go out to say goodbye to him. She stayed where she was, at the stove, making supper. When it was ready, she said, "I'm not hungry," and went upstairs to pack. I looked at the stir-fry and steamed rice and tried to remember what I'd had for lunch. I drew a blank. Adam and I hadn't gotten around to lunch. So I fixed a plate for myself and ate at the kitchen table, alone except for Shendor, who watched my fork move from plate to mouth to plate again. Dogs — I don't think it ever occurs to them *not* to hope.

I thought about Adam while I ate. He had been really rattled. After I cleaned up, I dialled his cell phone number. No service. He must have turned it off. I dialled the number I'd got out of the phone book last night. The same woman answered. I guessed it was Alison, B.J.'s mother. When I asked to speak to Adam, she said, "Just a moment." But it was her voice I heard again a few moments later, not Adam's. "I'm sorry," she said, "but he can't come to the phone right now. Would you like to leave a message?"

I left my name and number. I took the phone and the book David Mitchell had given me out onto the front porch, where I sat and read until the sun went down. I turned on the porch light and read some more. Adam didn't call.

My mother came downstairs around ten o'clock with her suitcase and a couple of tote bags filled with things she had been accumulating since spring break for my sister Brynn, who was sharing an apartment with a couple of other girls in Montreal. I took the bags from her and followed her to her SUV, where we stowed everything. After she locked the car, she said, "I'm going to bed."

"I don't think he really *wants* to stay," I said. "I think he'd much rather go with you."

"It's his choice," my mother said.

I wasn't so sure, but I didn't argue with her. In the first place, it wouldn't do any good. In the second place, I was afraid it would make her cry, and I didn't want to have to deal with that. So I said, "I know he'll catch up with you." She kissed me on the cheek and told me that she was planning to leave early. Then she went inside.

I went back to the porch. I thought about calling Adam's place again, but it was late. Besides, if he'd wanted to, he could have called me. Obviously he hadn't wanted to. Or hadn't been able to bring him-self to, which amounted to the same thing.

I was still out on the porch, book open on my lap, Shendor asleep at my feet, when Levesque's car pulled in. He looked up at the front window on the second floor, the window of the bedroom he shared with my mother. He stared at it for a while before he got out of the car and came up onto the porch. Shendor raised her head, but for once didn't get up to greet him. Maybe she was tired. Or maybe she sensed that he was.

"I thought you were going to Toronto," I said.

"I wanted to talk to Amanda Blake first."

"Does Jessie know?"

Levesque's face was solemn. "She knows that her father is dead. I don't know what else she's been told."

Poor Jessie.

Levesque glanced up at the window again.

"How's your mother?"

"Disappointed."

"Is she asleep?"

"She put her stuff in the car around ten and said she was going to bed. She's leaving first thing in the morning."

He tipped his head back a little and seemed to be listening for something. But there was nothing to hear.

"I'll be back tomorrow evening," he said.

"Then what?" I said.

He didn't answer. He didn't go inside, either.

chapter 11

I vaguely recall the door to my room opening. I vaguely recall the scent of my mother's after-shower body spray. I vaguely recall the jangle of Shendor's tags. So I'm pretty sure my mother must have poked her head in to say goodbye before she left. But I have no idea exactly what time it was when she got into her car and drove away.

I woke up at eight o'clock to find myself face-to-butt with Shendor, who would never think of lying on Mom and Levesque's bed, but who flopped down on mine every chance she got — which was one more reason to keep my bedroom door firmly closed at night. When I stirred, she raised her head and looked at me. When I rolled out of bed, she jumped down to the floor and made a beeline for the door.

I dressed, put some coffee on and let her out into the yard. She did what she had to do, raced back to the house, scratched at the door until I let her in, and nudged her food bowl from its place near the fridge over to the coffee machine where I was standing. I filled the bowl and settled down with a cup of coffee. The phone rang. It was Fletcher Blake. He said he was calling on behalf of Mrs. Blake. He said that, under the circumstances, she wouldn't need me today. He said he'd let me know when she might want me again. I told him that was okay. I asked him how Jessie was. His voice cracked a little when he said, "Devastated." I asked him to give her a hug for me and told him I was sorry about his brother.

I hung up the phone and sat down with my coffee.

The phone rang again.

I hoped it would be Adam.

It wasn't. It was someone whose voice I didn't recognize, asking to speak to the chief.

"He's not here," I said.

"This is Ed Winslow."

"Oh, hi, Mr. Winslow. This is Chloe. He's out of town. He won't be back until late tonight."

"Will you tell him I called? I guess it's not urgent, not with everything else that's been going on in town. But I'd appreciate hearing from him."

I promised I'd pass on his message.

After breakfast and a shower, I decided to head up to the lake to see if I could find Adam. I knew he was embarrassed by his reaction to finding Trevor Blake. I probably would have been too, if I'd done the same thing. In fact, I'd come pretty close. Not that long ago, *I* had been the first to stumble across a dead body. I hadn't fainted, but I had thrown up. The only difference was that I had been alone when it happened, so I'd been spared any embarrassment, but the experience gave me a pretty good idea how Adam must be feeling. And he was a guy, which probably made it worse.

The minute I reached for Shendor's leash on the hook inside the closet door, she was all over me, barking and jumping up. I made her sit and stay seated before I snapped the leash onto her collar. As soon as she heard it click, she sprang to her feet and charged the door. I made her sit again and stay seated before I opened the door. It's what my mother always did. "You have to set the ground rules for dogs and then stick to them," she said. My mother was the kind of person who never budged on ground rules.

While Shendor and I made our way into town, I thought about what my mother had said to Levesque. We had been living in Montreal when she met him. She'd been working as a waitress at a bar. The fiancé of one of her co-workers had been murdered and Levesque was assigned to the case. According to my mother, their first conversation had consisted of Levesque questioning her about the murder and my mother shaking and trying not to cry while she answered. After it was over, they had started going out. Pretty soon after that, she announced that they were going to get married. Not until yesterday had it occurred to me that she might have had some reservations about marrying a cop. His hours were bad. His schedule was unpredictable. And the work could be dangerous. Levesque had obviously smoothed over all of her objections. I could imagine it, based on what my mother had said. *I'm a homicide cop,* cherie, *the bad stuff is over by the time I get there. We'll move. Go someplace quiet.* But someplace quiet turned out to be someplace where Levesque had got shot.

Someplace where now a murder had pushed their long-delayed honeymoon off the rails. Was it going to have the same effect on their relationship? How angry was my mother that Levesque's sense of responsibility made him put his job ahead of her? Had that kind of dedication to his job been responsible for his first marriage breaking up? Would it push this one to the brink?

Shendor and I circled the north end of town and headed for the lake road. When we got there, I read the signs nailed to posts and trees that identified the owners of the cottages until I found one that said "Fuller." I followed the narrow dirt driveway through the trees, away from the road, until — *Wow!* — I spotted one of those not-really-a-cottage cottages. It was so well hidden by trees that you couldn't tell from the road, but this so-called cottage was a massive, eggshell blue house with a porch on all four sides and a deck on the second floor, overlooking the lake. It sat in the middle of a well-groomed lawn that sloped down to a boathouse and a dock where two boats were tied up — a sailboat and a cabin cruiser. There were three men on the dock. They didn't seem to notice me when I went up onto the porch and knocked on the door.

No answer.

I turned to look at the dock. One of the men — a tall guy with long black hair that hung in a thick braid down his back — was looking back at me. He must have said something because the other two turned to take a look. One of them, a chunky man

120

in a short-sleeved checked shirt and jeans, scowled. The third man, casually elegant in a white T-shirt and black slacks, started toward me. Bryce Fuller, Adam's father.

"Can I help you?" he said when he reached the top of the slope where I was standing.

"I'm looking for Adam."

He smiled benignly. "And you are?"

"I'm sort of a friend of his. We met in town."

"Ah. Well, he took his brother swimming."

I looked at the dock and the water that surrounded it, but I didn't see Adam or B.J.

"He took him to the beach," Mr. Fuller said. "He says B.J. is safer there. There's lots of shallow water and sand for B.J. to play in. He claims B.J. likes it better there." Something in his voice told me that Mr. Fuller suspected that Adam had other reasons for swimming at the public beach instead of at this private dock. He was probably right.

"I'm Bryce Fuller," he said, thrusting out a hand.

"Chloe," I said. He clasped my hand and shook it briskly, peering directly into my eyes the whole time.

"Adam mentioned you," he said. "Your father is chief of police here, isn't that right?"

I nodded. Mr. Fuller said how much he liked it up here and I said I did too. That seemed to exhaust the conversation between us, so I thanked him and left. When I glanced back over my shoulder from the end of the driveway, he was still standing on the slope, watching me.

The sun was high and hot by the time I got to the beach, which was littered with towels and beach umbrellas, bathing suits and bodies. I walked along the sand, my arm in full extension as Shendor did her best to drag me into the water and I did my best to resist. I scanned every face and every body before I spotted Adam. He was squatting near the edge of the water, shovelling sand into a bright red plastic bucket. B.J. sat cross-legged beside him. They were building a sand fort.

B.J. saw me and smiled, which made Adam look up. Up and right back down again.

I made Shendor sit. B.J. got up and approached her shyly, stopping at what he probably considered a safe distance.

"She's really friendly, B.J.," I said. "Hold out your hand. Let her smell you. That's how dogs get to know you."

He crept closer and extended a plump, brownish hand. Shendor sniffed it and then — sometimes you just have to love dogs — she extended a paw to him. He was instantly charmed. He laughed and came closer. Shendor must have been enjoying the attention because she didn't jump or bark or even stand up. She remained seated and let B.J. pat her. He giggled. Adam looked out over the lake.

I knelt down on the sand beside him. "I phoned you," I said. "I wanted to make sure you were okay."

He wouldn't even look at me.

"About what happened," I said. "It's no big deal. It's not every day that people find" — I glanced at

B.J. — "well, what we found. So when they do, they react in all kinds of ways — "

Adam stood up abruptly. "Come on, B.J. We'd better get back for lunch."

I stood up too.

"Adam, I don't care what happened. It doesn't matter."

"It matters to me," he said. He stooped to retrieve B.J.'s bucket and shovel, shoved a couple of beach towels into a backpack that was lying on the sand, and grabbed B.J. by the hand.

"I want to play with the dog," B.J. said.

"We have to go."

"Geez, Adam, so you fainted. So what?"

B.J. stared up at him in surprise. Adam glowered at me. He took B.J. roughly by the hand and yanked him away. B.J. yowled. He had to run to keep up with the pace Adam was setting. I watched his legs moving double-time and shook my head. Boy, some guys focus on all the wrong things. It was too bad, too, because at first I had been sure that Adam and I had a lot in common.

I was going to go home, but I thought about Jessie. Fletcher Blake had said she was devastated.

"Come on," I said to Shendor. We began the long trudge to Mrs. Blake's house.

Matt Solnicki answered the door. He had two black eyes and the knuckles of both hands were black and blue and swollen.

"Jessie isn't here right now," he said. "She's with her uncle."

"Will you tell her I stopped by?" I said.

"Who's at the door, Matt?" Mrs. Blake's voice called. She appeared beside him, her face pale, dark circles under her eyes. "Oh, Chloe."

"I'm so sorry about what happened," I said.

She seemed to be fighting back tears as she thanked me. "I was going to call you later," she said. "There are arrangements to be made." For the funeral, she meant. "I was wondering if you could come over tomorrow morning. Jessie would love to see you."

I said I would. I thought about Jessie all the way home. She was such a sweet kid. She had loved her father so much.

While I ate supper, I watched the local news. The Trevor Blake story was the lead, but there weren't many more details — just "murder investigation ongoing." The proposed new golf course was the second item. Bryce Fuller said in an interview that he had met with some members of the band council and was gratified to know that not everyone shared what he called David Mitchell's "radical and unreasonable point of view." He said that some members of the band council understood that a new golf course and more tourists spending more money in the area could benefit everyone. He said he hoped to pursue talks with a view to securing a win-win situation — whatever that meant.

* * *

Shendor's barking woke me up. At first it was wild and frantic. Then it stopped. I peered at the clock

124

on my bedside table — one-thirty in the morning. I got up and stumbled downstairs. A light was on in the kitchen. From the bottom of the stairs, I could see Shendor's tail thump-thump-thumping on the kitchen floor. Levesque was standing in front of the fridge, sniffing an open milk carton.

"It's still good," I said. "I had some in my coffee this morning."

He grabbed a glass from the cupboard and filled it with milk.

"Did your mother get away okay?" he said.

"I guess so. She was gone when I got up. You haven't talked to her?"

"I tried to get her on her cell phone."

Tried to get her.

"She hasn't called here?" he said.

I shook my head. Obviously she hadn't tried to get him on *his* cell, which meant that she wasn't happy with how things had turned out so far. He drank some milk. His shirt was wrinkled. He was still wearing a tie, but he had loosened it, and it hung crooked. He looked tired.

"Did you see that boy again? Adam?"

I nodded.

"Is he okay?"

"I don't know. He won't talk to me."

There was sympathy mixed with the exhaustion in his eyes. "At that age, a lot of boys haven't sorted out what's important and what isn't."

At that age? What about at Levesque's age?

"Do you think David Mitchell did it?" I said.

125

Levesque finished his milk, rinsed the glass and put it into the dishwasher, and didn't answer my question. Instead he said, "Were you at Mrs. Blake's today?"

"I dropped by. And she wants me for tomorrow while she makes arrangements for the funeral. Why?"

"I'm just wondering if it's a good idea for you to work for her right now."

"Why? You don't think *she* killed her ex-husband, do you?"

He just looked at me.

"David Mitchell is the most likely suspect, isn't he?" I said. He'd been in a couple of fights with Trevor Blake. He'd threatened him. They were on opposite sides of an important issue. And he'd been watching Trevor Blake in the park.

More silence.

"Mrs. Blake said that Jessie wanted to see me. We get along really great. And she just lost her father."

Levesque stared out the kitchen window for a few moments. He sighed as he turned back to me. "Okay," he said. "For now. Look, Chloe, I don't know what my schedule is going to be like for the next little while."

I wondered how many times he had said those same words to my mother.

"I'll be fine," I said.

* * *

"No big surprises," I heard Levesque saying early the next morning when I woke up. I crept out into the upstairs hall. His voice was coming from the kitchen. Was he talking on the phone? "One blow," he said. "Hammer."

Then I heard another voice. Steve Denby. He said, "Were they able to match it to the hammer we found in Blake's truck?"

Steve was down there with Levesque, which surprised me — not that he was in our kitchen, but that they were discussing business there. But then, Mom and Phoebe were out of town and, as far as Levesque knew, I was still asleep.

"So far all they said was *consistent with*," Levesque said. I knew what that meant — it meant that Trevor Blake could have been struck with the hammer that Levesque had found in Blake's truck, or he could have been struck with a hammer just like it. "But preliminary — there were traces of blood on the hammer."

"So whoever used it and wiped it clean wasn't thorough enough, " Steve said.

Wiped it clean of blood, I thought. And clean of fingerprints.

"That's assuming it's the murder weapon," Levesque said. He never assumed anything. "We should know soon if it's Blake's blood. They also said that the blow shattered the skull and drove fragments of bone into the brain. He probably died instantly. From the angle, it looks like the killer was left-handed." I thought about David Mitchell, standing at the front of my classroom with a pointer in his left hand, giving us a mini-history lesson.

"And the blow was inflicted from above and behind, so either the killer was taller or was standing on higher ground, or Blake was sitting or kneeling when he was hit."

"Or maybe in the water," Steve said, "with the killer on the boardwalk."

"Maybe," Levesque said. "But why would he be *in* the water?"

"Maybe he was killed somewhere else and dumped in the bog."

"He'd been dead maybe six or seven hours by the time Chloe found him, which means he was killed very early Sunday morning — say, six or seven o'clock," Levesque said. "Do we know what Blake was doing there?"

"He had a crew out there the day before, cleaning up that mess around the spruce bog. I talked to the guy who supervised the job. He said that Blake was going to check on the work first thing in the morning. Apparently he always checked up on his crews."

"I talked to his brother before I went down to Toronto," Levesque said.

"Fletcher Blake?" Steve said.

"Yes. He said Trevor had left the house by the time he woke up at seven, and hadn't returned by the time Fletcher left to pick up Mrs. Blake and Jessie at eight."

There was a pause. Then Steve said, "The terrain around the bog is flat and the ground is soft. If he'd been sitting or kneeling anywhere around there, we would have seen some evidence of that, wouldn't we? On his pants or on the ground. So he must have been either on the boardwalk or in the water when he was hit."

"Maybe."

Silence.

"If he was on the boardwalk, then the killer must be taller than Blake. Or Blake was bending over when the guy hit him."

"Guy?" Levesque said. "It could have been a woman."

"Trevor Blake is — was — a strong man. If a woman wanted to kill him, I don't think she'd use a hammer. Not unless he was already incapacitated — drunk or maybe drugged."

"We won't get toxicology results for at least a week," Levesque said. "And that's assuming they put a rush on it."

"It had to have been a man," Steve said. More silence. "I'm thinking David Mitchell or one of his guys. You said Chloe saw Mitchell in the park, watching Blake?"

I heard a sigh. Then Levesque said, "I'm going to go out and have a talk with him."

"Well, good luck," Steve said. "The OPP has really taken over. They have the area around the barricade contained and locked up tight. No one gets through. No one even gets near. They're not taking any orders from anyone around here. You should see how they're treating the station — like they own it."

I was willing to bet that was why Steve was at

our house, talking to Levesque in our kitchen.

"That fellow, Bryce Fuller?" Steve said. "Apparently he has friends in high places. Someone from the provincial legislature called Howard Eckler and told him that the premier expects everyone up here to co-operate fully with the OPP on the blockade situation. *And* that the OPP is reporting directly to Queen's Park on this one. It's like we don't even exist." He sounded indignant.

"I don't think they're going to give me any trouble," Levesque said. "This is a homicide investigation and I'm still chief of police here."

"Like I said, good luck," Steve said.

I heard a chair scrape back over the tile in the kitchen. I scurried back up the stairs as quietly as I could, darted across the upstairs hall and opened my bedroom door noisily before thumping down the stairs and pretending to be surprised when I saw Steve in the foyer, waiting for Levesque to gather his things.

"Hey, Steve," I said.

"Hey, Chloe."

"Is there coffee?"

"I think we left you some," Steve said.

Levesque glanced at me. "I don't know — "

"When you'll be back. I know. I'll be fine."

* * *

When I left the house, I told myself that it was going to be a difficult day, but that I could handle it. But the closer I got to Amanda Blake's house, the less confident I felt. What do you say to a little girl whose father has been murdered?

Mrs. Blake answered the door. She looked even paler and more exhausted than she had the day before, but she managed a wan smile.

"I really appreciate you coming over, Chloe," she said. "Jessie is out back in the tent. I shouldn't be gone more than a couple of hours."

I circled around to the back of the house, but hesitated when I reached the tent. I crouched down and called Jessie's name.

"In here," she said in a thin, quavering voice.

I pulled aside the flap and peeked inside. Jessie peered out at me. Her eyes were red from crying. As soon as I crawled in, she put her arms around me and started to cry again. I held her. I didn't know what else to do.

After a while she stopped crying, and I asked her if she wanted to go to the beach. She didn't. I asked if she wanted to watch TV. She didn't want to do that either. In the end, we took a bucket from the back porch and walked up toward the lake to look for berries. We found a thicket of raspberry bushes along the side of the road. A lot of them weren't ripe yet. I showed her how to look under the leaves to find the ones that were.

"Do you ever have dreams that are real?" Jessie said while she picked.

"Dreams that are real?" I'd lived a few nightmares — my one and only outing with a local loser named Rick Antonio sprang to mind — but I didn't think that was what she meant. "You mean, do I believe that dreams come true?" I wish. Someday my prince will come . . .

She shook her head as she dropped a couple of berries into the bucket. "I mean, when you dream something and you think it's real, but maybe it isn't."

"Well, some people sleepwalk. I read a story once about a guy who got up in the middle of the night and made himself some fried eggs and ate them. He made so much noise that his wife got up to see what was happening. She said he didn't say a word to her, he just ate his eggs and went back to bed. In the morning when she told him about it, he thought she was kidding. He didn't remember a thing about it." I didn't tell her that the wife had told this story in court, during her husband's trial, because one night he had got out of bed, driven across town and killed his sister-in-law. He claimed that he had been asleep at the time and that he didn't remember that, either. The jury didn't believe him.

Jessie thought for a moment and then shook her head. "This is different."

"What do you mean?"

"I was having a bad dream," she said. "About Daddy. And when I woke up, I had a bad feeling, so I went to Mom's room. But she wasn't there and I got scared. So I went downstairs and she wasn't there either. She was gone."

"Last night, you mean?"

She shook her head again. "The other night. I

went onto the couch and I fell asleep. In the morning, I woke up in bed. I asked Mom if she had put me there. She said she didn't know what I was talking about. She said I must have dreamed the whole thing because she was in her bed all night and she doesn't remember me going into her room. Then later that day, when we were in Toronto, Mom got a call. It was the police and they wanted her to go to a police station there." Probably Levesque had asked the Toronto police to contact her and tell her in person what had happened. "That's when we found out that Daddy had died." Tears welled up in her eyes again. "Do you think the dream I had was because of what was going to happen to my father?"

"Oh, I don't know, Jessie. People don't know everything there is to know about dreams. They're not sure why we dream the things we do or what our dreams mean."

"Mom said someone killed him," Jessie said in a small, trembling voice.

"I know."

"Mom said it was probably because of the golf course. She said if Daddy hadn't taken that job, he'd still be alive. She said Matt wouldn't have had that accident either."

I didn't know what to say.

"She said your dad is going to find out who did it."

"He will, Jessie."

"Promise?"

"It's his job, Jessie."

"Promise, Chloe?" A tear trickled down her cheek.

What could I say? "I promise."

We managed to fill half the bucket with raspberries and carried them back to Jessie's place. Mrs. Blake was home when we got there. She took me aside and told me that the funeral was the next day, so she wouldn't need me. She said she wasn't sure what she was going to do after that. What she really wanted was to take Jessie away for a while, but this was her busiest time of year and she wasn't sure that was going to be possible. If she couldn't get away, then she would probably want me to look after Jessie. But she just couldn't tell me for sure right now. I told her I'd wait to hear from her and that whatever she wanted to do was fine with me.

I was riding down the driveway when Fletcher Blake's van turned in. He stopped when he saw me and rolled down his window. He asked me how Jessie was. I told him.

"I hope your father's good at his job," he said.

I said he was and that he had worked plenty of homicide cases back in Montreal.

"Does he have any idea who could have done it? Has he found anything that might help him?"

I hesitated. I shouldn't really say anything. But there was nothing to say. I shook my head.

* * *

When I got home, I checked the phone for messages. There was just one, from my mother, calling to tell me — me, not Levesque — that she had arrived safely in Montreal. I wondered if Levesque had managed to get through to her. I flipped on the TV and tuned into the local *News at Five-thirty*. The lead story was the murder of Trevor Blake. The report was almost identical to the one broadcast the night before: "Police are still investigating." The second story, again, was the standoff between opponents and proponents of the new golf course. It looked like there were a couple of dozen OPP officers out at the blockade, all in what looked like riot gear. They must have been baking under those helmets and that body armour. Then a still shot of Levesque's face appeared on screen.

"There appears to be some tension between local authorities and the OPP over the situation out at the golf course site," the news reader said. Then the still picture vanished, replaced by a live-at-the-scene toothy blond woman holding a microphone. You could see the police barricade in the distance behind her and, farther back, the native barricade.

"East Hastings Police Chief Louis Levesque was observed in a heated conversation with Staff Sergeant Owen Nelson of the OPP earlier this afternoon," the reporter said. "Neither Chief Levesque nor Staff Sergeant Nelson will comment on the matter. But Chief Levesque was observed behind the native barricade around noon today. It is believed he was there to speak to protest organizer David Mitchell. There is some speculation that this was in connection with the murder of contractor

Trevor Blake, but neither Chief Levesque nor Staff Sergeant Nelson will confirm this."

I called Ross and asked him if he wanted to do something — anything.

"I'm already doing something," he said.

"Yeah? What?"

"I've got a story to cover."

"The standoff?"

I wasn't one hundred percent sure, but I think the sound I heard Ross make was a sigh.

"It's the Charpentier twins' birthday."

"Who are the Charpentier twins?"

"They're twins." Well, duh. "They've lived here forever."

"Forever?"

"Well, since they were born — in 1899."

"Geez, Ross, that would make them — "

"One hundred and six years old today. Which," Ross said, "makes them news. There's a party at the seniors' residence where they live."

"The seniors' residence with the crosswalk outside its front door, which you also covered?"

"Sometimes I just get lucky," Ross said. "Do you want to come? There'll be cake and ice cream."

I declined. Instead, I made a ham and Swiss cheese sandwich, with Dijon mustard, on rye bread. I wrapped it, slipped it into my bag, got Shendor's leash from the closet and walked her into town. I stopped at Benny's to pick up a container of coleslaw and another of milk. My next stop was the police station. I tied Shendor outside.

When I opened the police station door, half a dozen OPP officers — waiting to go on duty, I think — turned to look at me. One of them marched over to ask my business.

"She's my daughter," said a voice from somewhere behind a wall of blue Kevlar. I didn't see Levesque at first. Then he stood up and motioned me over to his desk, which was covered with photographs.

"I brought you something to eat," I said. I pulled out the sandwich, milk and coleslaw. He gathered up the photographs and set them aside before unwrapping his sandwich. "Those are from the scene, right?" I said.

He took a bite of ham and Swiss, and smiled. "Just like your mother makes," he said.

"She called." His face didn't show much, but I'd have been willing to bet that she hadn't phoned him. I'd also have been willing to bet that he hadn't got through to her yet either.

"How is she?"

I shrugged. "She's in Montreal." I glanced at the top photograph and immediately wished I hadn't. It was a full-colour shot of Trevor Blake's body, still in the water, with the boardwalk on one side and boggy water on the other.

"How's your sister?"

"Which one?" I said, even though I knew he was referring to Brynn.

"I know Phoebe's fine," he said. "She called a couple of days ago. I meant Brynn."

Phoebe adored Levesque. I got along with him okay, I guess. But Brynn didn't live with us so she didn't know him the way we did, and he hadn't got to know her well. I wondered how he felt about that.

"She's okay, I guess." I nudged the first photo aside so I could take a look at the next one. It had been taken facing south and showed the body, the boardwalk, the ground between the boardwalk and the drainage ditch and, beyond that, the road. "Mom didn't say."

"You didn't ask?"

"I didn't talk to her. She called when I was out. She left a message." I was trying to sneak a peek at the next picture when Levesque picked up the whole stack and dropped it into a drawer. Whatever. I'd already been up close and personal with the crime scene. "While Adam and I were waiting for you to arrive, I looked around." That earned me a sharp glance. "*Looked* around, not walked around," I said. "I didn't see anything." But then, I wasn't a police college graduate.

He stared off into space as he gulped down some milk. "Maybe you don't see anything," he said, more to himself, I think, than to me, "because there's nothing to see." He pulled open the drawer containing the photos and frowned down at the one on top.

"What do you mean?"

"What?" He looked up at me. "Thanks for the sandwich."

In other words: Run along, like a good girl.

chapter 12

Levesque had planned to go to the funeral with me, but five minutes before we were due to leave — me in a black skirt and dark grey tank top, him in uniform — the phone rang.

"I'll drop you on the way," he said after he hung up.

"On the way where?"

"I have to go out to the barricade."

I could have asked why, but I probably wouldn't have got an answer. So I didn't bother.

Trevor Blake must have known a lot of people because the church was packed. I took a seat somewhere near the middle. A few minutes later Ross slid in beside me.

"Are you covering this?" I said.

He shook his head. "A couple of years ago when I had a paper route, I delivered the *Beacon* to both Mr. Blake and Mrs. Blake's houses. He never paid on time, but she did. She was a good tipper too, especially at Christmas."

Mrs. Blake was sitting in the front row. I saw the top of Jessie's head beside her. Matt Solnicki sat on the other side of Jessie. Off to one side, Fletcher Blake sat grim-faced in his wheelchair. Throughout the service, Mrs. Blake dabbed at her eyes with a tissue. At one point, Fletcher Blake spoke about his brother. When he said what a good father he had been, Jessie started to cry. Mrs. Blake drew her close and said something into her ear. Jessie clung to her mother.

When the service was over, six pallbearers walked alongside the coffin to the back of the church. Fletcher Blake followed immediately after them. In his wake were Jessie, Mrs. Blake and Matt Solnicki. I turned toward the back of the church to watch them — and spotted a familiar face in the crowd. Derek Lloyd. When Mrs. Blake got close to him, he took one of her hands in his and said something to her. She looked surprised to see him.

"I guess the murder must have made the news in Toronto," I said.

"Huh? What makes you say that?" Ross said, looking around at the mourners, the vast majority of whom appeared to be local.

"See that guy over there?" I pointed at Derek Lloyd. "He lives in Toronto. As far as I know, he doesn't know anyone up here except Mrs. Blake. And she looks surprised to see him, so he must have found out about the funeral from the Toronto papers."

"Or from the local news," Ross said. "Or from Fletcher Blake."

"He only met Fletcher Blake once, at Mrs. Blake's house. And I already told you, he's not local."

"First of all, he is local, at least for the summer. And second, I saw him — his name is Lloyd, right?" I nodded. "I saw Mr. Lloyd talking to Fletcher

Blake in town. They were having a pretty intense conversation."

"They were?" But they barely knew each other. "When was this?"

"The day after I did my interview with Fletcher Blake. I ran into him and Mr. Lloyd at the gas station. Mr. Blake told Mr. Lloyd about the interview. He said I'd done a terrific job." Ross puffed up with pride. "And Mr. Lloyd told me himself that he was on his way to a place north of Morrisville."

He had told Mrs. Blake that he'd been looking at places up there. When he'd decided not to take a place down here, he must have taken one up there instead.

"He's kind of a jumpy guy, isn't he?" Ross said.

"He is?"

"He kept looking around, like he was expecting someone, but not in a good way."

I remembered how he'd reacted when Mrs. Blake had mentioned her ex-husband.

"And he was having an intense conversation with Fletcher Blake? Do you have any idea what they were talking about?"

Ross made a sour face. "I don't eavesdrop on people, Chloe."

"But you're a reporter. Doesn't that go with the territory?"

He was not amused.

* * *

The next day, when neither Mrs. Blake nor Fletcher Blake called to tell me that I was needed,

I decided to start looking for another job — just in case. I couldn't spend the summer doing nothing. I went into every retail outlet in town — the drugstore, clothing stores, the Book Nook, Canadian Tire, the supermarket, Benny's — and every restaurant, even Big Putt Miniature Golf, and asked if they were hiring. A few places let me fill out applications, but everyone said the same thing: we can't make any promises.

By noon I was discouraged — and directly across the street from the *Beacon* office, which was located in a Victorian-era house at the west end of Centre Street. Maybe Ross was ready for lunch. Maybe we could grab a bite together. I crossed the street and pushed open the front door.

Most of the ground floor of the house had been converted to crowded open-concept office space. Eight battered desks, all but one of them unoccupied, were divided from each other by a rat's nest of computer and electrical cables and stacks of bundled newspapers — the current issue of the *Beacon*? Back issues? Near the back of the open area, behind a counter, sat Mrs. Torelli, who was the *Beacon*'s advertising sales manager. Beyond the counter were two glass-walled offices. One of them belonged to Mr. Torelli. The other was for Mrs. Torelli, but I had never seen her in it. She seemed to prefer sitting at the counter where she had a view of the whole place. Mr. Torelli wasn't in his office today either. He was standing beside Mrs. Torelli, looking blandly at a man who was giving him an earful.

"You people in the media cause most of the trouble," the man was saying when I arrived. He had long, silver, braided hair and was dressed plainly in faded jeans and a short-sleeved shirt. Although I had seen him around, I didn't know his name. But I did know that he was a member of the band council. "If you'd done your homework," he said, "you'd know that David Mitchell isn't radical and irresponsible. He always keeps a cool head. He calms things down; he doesn't stir them up. If it weren't for him, there would have been blood shed last year over that logging dispute. David Mitchell was the peacemaker in that."

Peacemaker? He and a group of armed men were manning the barricade out near Allendale. He was on record as saying that native people had to be prepared to defend their rights by any means possible. What did that have to do with making peace?

"Actually," Mr. Torelli said, "it was Bryce Fuller who said he was irresponsible. We merely quoted him."

"Quoted *him*," the man said. "What about the other side? Aren't you people supposed to be objective?"

Mrs. Torelli spotted me and eased her way past her husband. She picked her way through a maze of desks and newspaper bundles toward me.

"Can I help you?" she said.

"I'm looking for Ross."

She gave me a mournful expression. What was that about?

"He went to lunch," she said.

"You people make me sick," the man with the plaited hair said.

Mrs. Torelli sighed. "Excuse me," she said, and headed back to the counter. "Now, Mr. Bird," she said, "we would welcome an opinion article on the situation, if you would be interested in writing one. Isn't that right, Anthony?"

Mr. Torelli nodded, but without much enthusiasm.

"I don't want to write an *opinion* article," Mr. Bird said. "I just want you people to do your job. Report the facts. Tell *both* sides of the story for a change."

He wheeled around and stalked out of the office.

I went looking for Ross.

I found him in a booth at Stella's. He looked glummer than I had ever seen him.

"Are you okay?" I said, slipping into the booth opposite him.

"Remember that interview I did with Fletcher Blake?"

"Sure." How could I forget? "The highlight of your career so far, right?"

"Right," Ross said. "Interviewing Fletcher Blake was like . . . like interviewing the new Yousuf Karsh."

"If you say so."

He gave me a withering look. "You have no idea who Yousuf Karsh is, do you?"

"Well — "

He snorted in exasperation. "What's wrong with people in this town? Yousuf Karsh was only the most famous portrait photographer who ever worked in this country."

Okay, so he was in that kind of mood. "What happened, Ross?" He glowered at me. "Maybe I don't know anything about photography," I said. "But that doesn't mean I don't care about your problems. Come on. What's the matter?"

Ross looked at me for a moment before finally saying, "I taped a two-hour interview with Fletcher Blake. I took the tape back to the office. But before I could get a chance to transcribe it, I got assigned a *story*." His tone made it clear that he was using the word *story* loosely, the same way some people use the word *sport* to refer to curling or bowling. "And, of course, that story had to be written up immediately."

"The crosswalk story?"

"The Sanderson story."

"Sanderson?"

That earned me another snort of exasperation. "Do you ever even glance at the *Beacon?*"

"Well — "

"Even if you did, you probably wouldn't have read the Sanderson story," Ross said, sounding even more annoyed. "You're not the human-interest type. The Sandersons have been married forever."

"Kind of like the Charpentiers, huh?"

Another withering look. "The Charpentiers are sisters."

"Twins," I said, so he couldn't accuse me of not having listened to him. "How long is forever, anyway?"

"In the Sandersons' case, sixty-five years. Which means I had to go and cover their stupid wedding anniversary — and take pictures of them and their cake. Then I had to write it up, fast, so it would make the next edition because of course you wouldn't want to go to press without *that* story."

"I guess the life of a reporter isn't all it's cracked up to be, huh?"

"I did the Blake interview last Thursday. I left the tape on my desk. At least, I thought I did. Then, what with Matt Solnicki's car accident and the barricade and Trevor Blake's murder, well, everything got pretty crazy. Mr. Torelli had me running all over town, taking pictures and covering stories that he and the regular reporters usually cover, only they weren't doing that because they were covering all the really big stories. And Mr. Torelli even let some of those out-of-town journalists use the office for phone calls and e-mail. It wasn't until today that I had time to even think about transcribing my tape. That's when I discovered it was gone."

"Gone?"

"I looked all over for it. When I finally told Mr. Torelli it was missing, do you know what he said?"

I didn't, so I waited.

"He said that *he* had taken it."

"Mr. Torelli, you mean?"

Ross nodded. "He said Mr. Blake — "

"Fletcher Blake?"

He nodded again. "Fletcher Blake came to the office yesterday afternoon and asked Mr. Torelli when the interview was going to appear in the paper. Mr. Torelli told him he wasn't sure because of everything that was happening in town. He said that Mr. Blake understood completely. He said he was very nice about it. Then Mr. Blake said that he didn't do many interviews and wanted to know if he could listen to the tape."

I was still waiting for him to get to the point.

"So Mr. Torelli gave my tape to Mr. Blake."

"Gave it to him?"

"So that Mr. Blake could make a copy."

It didn't sound like the end of the world to me, but Ross seemed to think it was.

"It was *my* tape, Chloe. It was *my* interview. I would have been happy to give him a copy, *after* I had a chance to listen it."

"He's going to give it back, isn't he?"

He gave me another sharp look.

"Not that that's the point," I said quickly. Then I had a thought. "What if Mr. Blake listens to the tape and decides he doesn't like something he said?"

"Bingo," Ross said.

"You took notes, right, Ross?" Ms Peters, the teacher advisor for our school newspaper, was always telling us not to rely on technology and to be sure to take notes. A lot of kids thought that was because she probably had to call in her twelve-year-old nephew to reset her computer or program her VCR.

Ross looked glum all over again, which told me that he hadn't taken notes. Ms Peters went up a notch in my estimation.

* * *

After Ross went back to work — he said he was going to write down everything he could remember about the interview — I meandered through town. When I passed the police station, I saw that the parking lot was full of OPP cruisers. It looked as if they had taken over the place, just like Steve had said. As I was going by, Levesque came out the rear door looking as grim-faced as Ross. He got into his patrol car and was turning onto Elgin when he spotted me. He rolled down his window and said, "Get in."

"What did I do now?"

"Just get in, Chloe."

I climbed into the front seat and buckled up.

"Let's take a drive," he said.

Let's take a — "You mean a driving lesson?" I said. "Don't you have a murder to solve?"

He gave me the same sort of sharp look that I had got from Ross. "I need a break."

Some people find a few hours devoted to stamp collecting to be the pause that refreshes. Others unwind by playing a few rounds of the exacting so-called sport of lawn bowling. So it should have come as no surprise that there was at least one person on the planet whose idea of decompression was watching someone else get all tense at the prospect of having to parallel park.

"You're going to let me drive a police car?" I said.

His look said *Don't be ridiculous,* even if he didn't. "Ed will have something we can use."

Ed Winslow.

Oh-oh.

"Um, I forgot to tell you. He called the other day." I cringed in my seat and prayed that Levesque wasn't in as bad a mood as he seemed to be.

"He? Ed Winslow?"

I nodded.

"Which other day?"

"Monday."

"Monday?" He glanced at me, annoyed. "That was three days ago."

"Well, he said it wasn't urgent."

"What else did he say?"

"Just that he'd appreciate hearing from you."

He looked even more annoyed now. "Do I ever forget to give you a message?"

I know a rhetorical question when I hear one. I didn't answer.

"Well?" he said. "Do I?"

Okay, so it one of *those* rhetorical questions, the kind that parents and teachers like to make kids answer, purely to humiliate them. "No, but — "

"There are no excuses."

Of course not.

There was no mercy either. Ed Winslow was sitting out in front of the rusted trailer that served as his office — or maybe his house — when he saw Levesque's car. He stood up, not smiling, when Levesque stopped the car and killed the engine. Levesque turned to me.

"You owe the man an apology," he said.

I sighed and got out of the car.

"Hi, Mr. Winslow."

Mr. Winslow nodded curtly.

"I'm really sorry, Mr. Winslow, but when you gave me that message a couple of days ago, well, um — " Spit it out, I told myself. Get it over with. "I kind of forgot to pass it along." Two stern pairs of eyes were fixed on me now — Ed Winslow's and Levesque's. "But we're here now," I said, desperate to locate the silver lining in this embarrassing black cloud.

"I'm sorry, Ed," Levesque said. "Chloe said" — he turned his sharp eyes on me again — "that you wanted to talk to me."

Mr. Winslow disappeared inside the trailer, banging the door closed after him. Levesque glanced at me. I looked at the toes of my sandals and made a mental note to touch up my nail polish. The trailer door opened again and Mr. Winslow came out carrying a brown paper bag. He handed it to Levesque.

Levesque opened it and looked inside.

"I found them in the garbage," he said.

I glanced around the yard, which was filled with rusting vehicles, mounds of old tires, all kinds of car and truck parts, and miscellaneous other scrap, and wondered what was garbage and what wasn't, and how he knew the difference.

"You think these have something to do with what happened to Skipper?" Levesque said.

"Well, they're not mine and I didn't put them there. I'm the only person who's here regular. And I don't recall any of my customers" — I still found it hard to believe that he actually had customers or that anyone could make a living, even a modest one, running a junkyard — "wearing them. And they're not the kind of thing that you'd miss. If a person was wearing those, you'd notice. *I'd* notice. They were near the bottom of a trash can out back. I found 'em when I was emptying it and I remembered you saying to the other fellow" — he probably meant Steve — "that you didn't find any fingerprints. I figure maybe that's why. Whoever poisoned Skipper and took that car was wearing those. Probably thought I'd never notice. Probably thought I couldn't tell garbage from good junk." He glanced at me. I felt my cheeks burn.

"You could be right," Levesque said.

"I don't suppose you'll be able to do anything with them though, will you?" Mr. Winslow said.

"You never know, Ed," Levesque said. "I'll keep you posted." He glanced at me. "Get back in the car, Chloe."

Geez, get in the car, get out of the car. You'd think my name was Skipper. But I got in and so did Levesque, and the next thing I knew he was backing up the car.

"I thought you were going to borrow a car for my driving lesson."

"I've got to take care of this first."

"What did he give you?"

No answer.

I reached for the bag, which Levesque had set on the floor at my feet. He didn't stop me. All he said was, "Don't touch what's inside."

I opened the bag and peeked in. "You have to be kidding," I said. The bag contained a pair of bright yellow rubber gloves, the kind you use when you're scrubbing the toilet. "Even if Mr. Winslow is right and whoever stole the car and poisoned Skipper was wearing these, how are they going to help? The whole point of these is that they don't leave finger-prints, right?"

Of course I got no answer.

We were on our way back into town when Levesque got a call from Steve. He said, "The OPP just arrested David Mitchell."

Levesque said, "Did something happen out at the barricade?"

"No," Steve said. "They arrested him for the murder of Trevor Blake."

chapter 13

"You're going to have to get home on your own," Levesque said.

There were a lot of people milling around on the sidewalk outside the police station. I knew a few of them personally and recognized most of the others. Local people. Maybe some of the summer people noticed that a resident of East Hastings had been murdered. Maybe they noticed that one of the roads was blockaded. But it was a safe bet that very few of them knew who Trevor Blake was and still fewer cared that they couldn't get to the end of a road that, at the moment, went nowhere. But for local people — well, it was big news.

There were quite a few media gathered in front of the police station. I counted four different camera crews, as well as people carrying tape recorders and microphones — radio people, I guessed. There was also a bunch of reporters who were equipped with mini-recorders and notebooks and who looked grungier than the well-groomed TV types. They were the print journalists.

Levesque parked the car and headed to the rear door of the police station. I went straight for the action. I'd spotted Ross in the crowd when we drove past and I sought him out now.

"Covering this for the *Beacon*?" I said.

"Are you kidding?" he said. He sounded angry.

"Mr. Torelli's here. He takes all the best stories for himself. I'm just the photographer." He held up a camera.

"Don't even think about pointing that thing at me, Ross."

"You know what he told me?"

I didn't. But I knew I was going to find out.

"He told me, take lots of pictures. He said if I take enough, he should be able to find *something* usable. Nothing like having confidence in your reporters."

"He probably didn't mean anything by it, Ross. He's probably just being practical. Besides, even really good photographers do the same thing."

"*Even?*" Ross said.

"Digital cameras make it easier and cheaper to take a *lot* of pictures. That's why Fletcher Blake says he likes them so much."

Ross flinched when I mentioned that name. It was obviously still a sensitive topic.

"Sorry," I said.

A hum went through the crowd. People started to press forward. Ross wormed his way toward the front door of the police station. I followed closely behind and watched while he took picture after picture of the men who were coming out. There were three of them — the same three men I had seen on the dock at Adam's place. Two of them — the native man with the thick braid, and the chunky white guy — stayed as far from the reporters as they could and kept their mouths shut. The third, Bryce Fuller, wasn't as media-shy. He didn't seem to mind being mobbed by reporters. He looked calm as he spoke to them. I didn't catch everything he said, but it had something to do with the golf course.

Not so calm was another man who was trying to catch the attention of the media. It was Mr. Bird, the man I had heard talking to Mr. Torelli when I'd gone to the *Beacon* office to look for Ross. He pressed in among the reporters, grabbing first one and then another by the arm and trying to talk to them. I heard him say the same word over and over again — *peacemaker*.

But the reporters all focused on Bryce Fuller. They followed him as he led the other two men through the crowd to the street, where they got into a Lexus SUV and drove away. Even then Mr. Bird didn't manage to buttonhole more than a couple of reporters, and I didn't think they were going to report much of what he said. I turned out be to right. He didn't make the TV news or any newspaper that I saw later that day.

The crowd waited a little longer, but no one else came out of the police station and nothing else happened. Then, because it was getting late, a lot of the media people left. I bet they all went out to the barricade to see what was happening there.

I looked for Ross and found him standing on the sidewalk, staring intently at his camera. When I crept up behind him, I saw that he was peering into the camera's display, reviewing the photos he had taken. He held the camera out so that I could see.

"I'd say there are a *lot* of pretty good pictures here, wouldn't you?" he said.

"Did you hear anything?" I said. "What made them arrest David Mitchell?"

I remembered how surprised I had been to see him in the park instead of at the barricade on Saturday. I remembered that he had been watching Trevor Blake. If he'd been responsible for the tree I had nearly collided with, and for driving Mr. Solnicki and me off the road, then killing Trevor Blake would be just one more way to try to stop the golf course from being built. They were hardly the actions of a peacemaker but, boy, were they ever consistent with someone who was on record as saying that he was prepared to use any means necessary to protect native rights.

"Someone saw him leaving the barricade in the middle of the night on Saturday," Ross said. According to Levesque, Trevor Blake had been killed between six and seven on Sunday morning. "Someone else — actually, I think someone said it was a couple of guys — said they heard Mitchell talking about wanting to get even with Trevor Blake."

"Someone? Who?"

"I don't know. But I heard it was a couple of native guys."

That didn't sound good for David Mitchell.

"David Mitchell is left-handed, and Mr. Torelli said that the blow that killed Trevor Blake was made by someone who is left-handed," Ross said.

I couldn't imagine Levesque leaking that particular piece of information. So how did Mr. Torelli know? Maybe he was a better journalist than I gave him credit for.

"*And* Lyle Turnbull said that he drove through the park a little before six on Sunday morning and that he saw David Mitchell's car on the road near where the body was found."

"Lyle Turnbull?"

"One of the guys who came out of the police station with Bryce Fuller," Ross said. "The white guy. He's a contractor."

"That was enough to arrest Mitchell?"

"I think the clincher was Maurice Dumont."

"Who?"

"The other guy with Bryce Fuller. The native guy. He's on the band council. Apparently he also drove through the park early that morning. I heard someone say that Dumont claims he saw Mitchell throwing something into the back of a pickup truck that was parked at the side of the road."

"A dark blue pickup?" Trevor Blake's truck.

Ross looked surprised. "How did you know?"

"It's a long story." One that involved two associates of Bryce Fuller — associates who both just happened to be driving through the park before six on Sunday morning — pointing the finger at David Mitchell. The same Bryce Fuller who was probably dying to get Mitchell out of the way so that he could build his golf course. What had David Mitchell said to Levesque on our porch? *Are you sure Bryce Fuller's people didn't do it to make us look bad?* I remembered what Adam had told me — that his father would do anything to make money. Bryce Fuller's past was full of flashy developments, fast deals and big money. And what about David Mitchell's past? People said it was full of trouble.

People said . . . On the ridge overlooking the bog, David Mitchell had asked me, What do you know about me?

"There's something you're not telling me, Chloe," Ross said. "What is it?"

I looked at the camera in his hand and the tape recorder he always had with him these days. He was a journalist. He didn't get the big assignments, not with Mr. Torelli as a boss. But he took his job seriously. If I told him anything, he'd feel obligated to do something about it, to follow it up or to tell Mr. Torelli, which made Ross pretty much the last person I should be talking to.

"I'll tell you," I said. "Under two conditions."

He waited.

"One, this is strictly between you and me. If you tell anyone or use anything I say, we're not friends any more. Ever."

Ross nodded. "And two?"

"Two, you have to do something for me. Right now."

* * *

The sun beat down on my head as I trudged home after spending an hour and a half at the *Beacon* office with Ross. He had done a number of online searches for me, had uncovered a lot of information and had printed the good stuff out for me. As he retrieved the last few sheets of paper from the printer, he said, "Is this part of the strictly-between-you-and-me deal, or can I use this?"

"What would you do with it?"

"Maybe show it to Mr. Torelli. You know, so he can maybe do an article that's a little more — "

"Balanced?"

"Maybe. Chloe, right from the beginning, all I've heard about David Mitchell is that he's a real hot-head and that he's been in a lot of trouble with the law. I think that's all anyone has heard. But this stuff — " He waved at the stack of paper in my hand. "Well, when you look at what's really happened, you get a different picture of the guy. You sure don't get the idea that he'd run anyone off the road or that he'd murder someone."

Ross had a point. When I'd first heard Mr. Bird defend David Mitchell, I thought he was biased — one native guy defending another native guy. But the couple of dozen newspaper articles we had found shed a different light on things.

"If you think it will do any good, use it," I said. "But you can't use anything I told you about Trevor Blake or about Adam and me finding him. Okay?"

"I promise," Ross said.

I chose to believe him.

I was at the bottom of my street, wondering what I was going to do with what we had found, wondering if it made any difference, when a car horn tooted and a Suzuki SUV pulled even with me. The driver, looking very sharp in designer sunglasses, peered at me as he slowed the vehicle. The passenger-side window slid down. The driver leaned toward it and said, "Any chance you'd accept an apology?" When I hesitated, he said, "To answer your question, yes, I know I acted like a jerk. And yes, I know it was stupid. I have this one small flaw — well, okay, so maybe I have more than one. But the one that seems to have been in play this time was that perennial favourite — stupid male pride."

I couldn't help myself. I laughed. When I did, he smiled.

"I really am sorry," Adam said. "I felt like an idiot. I mean, I'm on the football team at school. *And* the hockey team. I have my lifeguard qualifications. I passed all the tests — you know, how to save people, how to administer artificial respiration. I have my first-aid certification. And what happens? I stumble across a body" — I don't think I imagined a shudder when he said it — "and what do I do? First I faint dead away. Then I wake up to find I've had an accident. And to top it all off, I take one more look at the body and, well, I don't have to remind you. You were there. I was embarrassed. Maybe I shouldn't have been, but I was." He pulled off his sunglasses and looked into my eyes. "So how about it? Forgive me?"

"There's nothing to forgive, Adam," I said. "There never was."

"So get in. Let's do something. I'll buy you supper."

160

I thought about the sheaf of articles in my bag. I thought about how late it would be before Levesque got home. Then I looked at Adam, who was waiting for my answer.

"Okay," I said. "But I can't stay out for long. There's something I have to do."

We drove into town and ate at Stella's. Adam was back to his fun, talkative self and we had a great time. It got even better when Adam drove me home. He pulled up out of sight of the house, leaned over and kissed me. I kissed him back.

* * *

Shendor didn't run barking to the door to greet me. She was too busy quivering with pleasure because Levesque was scratching behind her ear. I'm not sure he even knew he was doing it, because he was talking on the phone at the same time. He glanced at me when I came into the kitchen, then shifted his attention back to the phone and said, *"Moi aussi, cherie."*

Oh. He was talking to my mother. Whenever he said anything, he said it softly and in French, which experience had taught me was a good sign. When he and my mother were being quiet together, they always spoke French. My mother's French had improved dramatically since she and Levesque had been married.

I watched him as he stood near the sink. A gentle breeze ruffled the curtain and Levesque smiled. He liked living in the country where, he claimed, it always got cool at night and where you didn't have

161

to bother with air conditioning. Then the doorbell rang. If you had given me a hundred chances to guess who was at the door, I still wouldn't have come up with the right answer.

"Hello, Chloe," said one of the two men standing on the porch.

"Mr. Lawry, hello." I hadn't seen my history teacher since school had ended. I had *never* seen him dressed like this before, in shorts, white athletic socks pulled up to mid-calf and Birkenstocks.

The man with him was Mr. Bird.

"Is your dad in, Chloe?" Mr. Lawry said. I started to nod when Mr. Lawry looked over my shoulder and said, "Louis, sorry to bother you at home. We checked the station first, but — "

"Don't apologize, Gerry," Levesque said. He handed me the cordless phone. "Your mother wants to have a word with you."

"I'll call her back," I said.

"Now," Levesque said.

I had no choice. I took the phone from him and went inside while he stepped out onto the porch. I hovered just inside the front door and only half-listened to what my mother was saying. Mostly I was straining to find out why my history teacher had come to my house. I heard David Mitchell's name mentioned.

After my mother had told me about everyone she had visited so far — most of them friends of hers whom I didn't care much about — she quizzed me on how things were going at home. I kept it simple:

I said, "Fine." She didn't push for details, probably because Levesque had already filled her in on the important stuff.

By the time I hung up, Levesque was back in the house and Mr. Lawry and Mr. Bird were gone.

"What was that about?" I said.

"There was a message for you when I got home," Levesque said. "Mrs. Blake wants to know if you can stay with Jessie tomorrow. You'd better call her."

After I phoned Mrs. Blake, I said, "Remember what you told me about David Mitchell?"

Levesque gave me a look that said he didn't want to get into it with me.

"When this whole thing started," I said, "you told me that David Mitchell had been arrested a lot of times and that he'd even served some time. Well, I did some research. And, yeah, he did some time. But most of the arrests were for minor stuff — for supposedly trespassing on land that native people claim as theirs, for refusing to disperse during a protest, that kind of thing."

Levesque gave me a stern look. I could imagine what he was thinking — the law is the law.

"A couple of articles said the same thing that I heard Mr. Bird tell Mr. Torelli — that when David Mitchell shows up at a standoff, he always calms things down. That he's a good negotiator and that he stops violence; he doesn't start it."

Levesque's face showed no reaction. It was time to tell him what I had found out. "As far as I could find out, he was only arrested three times on serious charges. The first time, assaulting a police officer."

"Chloe — "

"Hear me out," I said. "It happened in Quebec where some native people were staging an occupation to try to stop a condo development on land they claimed as theirs. David Mitchell managed to get a lot of local support. It looked like his side was going to win. Then the cops stopped allowing the native women to bring food to the protesters. When the women tried to get through anyway, the cops stopped them with force. Two women were hurt, which is when David Mitchell intervened. He was trying to protect them. He got arrested. A couple of days later, the protest collapsed.

"The second time was a logging dispute. Natives claimed the right to log on Crown lands. David Mitchell was handling the negotiations. Then one night the place where he was staying was burned down. His sister was in the house at the time. She suffered third-degree burns to both arms. The next day, according to some native people, two white guys told Mitchell that there'd be more fires if he didn't back off. Mitchell swung at them and ended up getting arrested for assault. It took months before there was a full investigation of the fire. It turned out it was arson, but no one was ever arrested — well, except David Mitchell, for assault.

"The third and last time — "

"Was the fisheries dispute," Levesque said. I

stared at him. "The natives in that case asked Mitchell to help them negotiate with the government. The other side didn't want him there. They tried to pick a fight with him in a bar. Mitchell stayed calm, but the guy he was with threw a punch. Mitchell only got involved when it looked like the white guys were going to beat his friend to death. When it was over, the white guys pressed charges and Mitchell was arrested. He'd be locked up now if the bartender — a white guy — hadn't come forward and told the police what really happened. The charges were dropped. Six months later the bar closed down — after a boycott by the white community."

I should have known.

The doorbell rang again.

"I'll get it," I said, glad for any excuse to get out of there. Shendor raced me to the door. It was Steve. I let him in and pointed him to the kitchen. I followed him.

"They're arraigning David Mitchell tomorrow," he said. "While you were out at the barricade, Nelson informed me that the OPP has taken over the investigation." He meant Staff Sergeant Owen Nelson of the OPP.

"I know," Levesque said.

"They've taken over everything to do with Mitchell. They make me feel like I don't belong at my own desk. You know what Nelson had me doing? Running out to get sandwiches for him and his men. I had to get out of there."

Levesque's expression was unreadable. He glanced over Steve's shoulder at me.

"Would you like a cup of coffee, Steve?" I said. "I could make some, no problem."

"Sure, that'd be — "

"Run along, Chloe," Levesque said.

Run along. As if I were six years old instead of sixteen.

I scooped up my book, which was sitting on the kitchen table, and went out onto the front porch. I waited until I heard the kitchen door close behind me and then I circled around to the kitchen window where I could listen. I figured I was entitled. I had found the body. Well, actually, Adam had found it. But I'd been with him at the time. I was the reason he had been in that part of the park.

"It's a temporary situation, Steve," Levesque was saying. "It happens. Things like this get political. They shouldn't, but they do."

There was silence for a few moments before Steve said, "The Solnicki incident — are we treating that as related to the Trevor Blake murder?"

"We haven't made a definite link between the two yet," Levesque said. "Why?"

There were another few beats of silence.

"Those gloves you gave me? I got two clear prints from the inside of them," Steve said. "Right thumb and left index finger. I ran them through AFIS."

"And?"

"I got a match. Trevor Blake."

"*What?*"

"The prints I recovered from the inside of the gloves were Trevor Blake's. The thing is, I didn't mention it to Nelson."

Levesque didn't say anything.

"You know why Blake is on record at AFIS?"

"Assault," Levesque said. "Six years ago. Winnipeg. The complainant was Amanda Blake. Just the one assault and the one conviction. He got a suspended sentence, mostly thanks to her intervention."

"Yeah," Steve said. He sounded a little deflated.

"Good work, Steve. It's not easy to get useable prints off the inside of a pair of rubber gloves."

I pictured Steve perking up again.

"I also checked with Ed Winslow," Steve said. "He said Trevor Blake had been out to his place a few times and made a few purchases. But he swears Blake hasn't been out there in the past few months."

"Those gloves didn't crawl into that garbage can all by themselves," Levesque said.

"There was some dried matter on one of the gloves. I'm not positive, but it looked like dried meat of some kind. Maybe hamburger. I talked to the vet who looked at Skipper. The dog died after eating poisoned hamburger meat. So I sent the glove down to the veterinary college. They'll do an analysis for us, but it'll take a couple of days."

"So," Levesque said, "Trevor Blake's fingerprints are in a pair of gloves that might also have on them residue of the poisoned meat that killed Ed

Winslow's dog, on the same night that someone broke into Ed's place and *borrowed* the vehicle that drove Matt Solnicki off the road."

If it were me, I would have jumped right to the conclusion: Trevor Blake had been driving that vehicle. Trevor Blake had driven me off the road. I could have been killed — by Trevor Blake. By Jessie's father.

Levesque didn't make that leap. Not yet. He always said you had to keep an open mind until all the facts were in. He said if you didn't, you developed tunnel vision, and that tunnel vision is one of the main reasons why innocent people get arrested and even convicted.

"Say, for the sake of argument," he continued, "that it was Trevor Blake who drove Matt Solnicki off the road. Why would he do that?" Before Steve could answer, Levesque started ticking off some possible links. "Solnicki was contracted to do some work on the golf course, wasn't he? Do we know if there was any friction between him and Blake? Solnicki has been seeing Blake's ex-wife, hasn't he? Is there anything there?"

"The Blakes were divorced before they moved here," Steve said.

"That's unusual, don't you think? A divorced couple moving to the same town together and living, what, maybe a kilometre from each other? Especially when she once pressed charges against him for assault."

"That was a long time ago," Steve said. "Apparently he went through an anger-management program. And he wanted to stay involved in his daughter's life. From everything I've ever seen or heard, they've managed the relationship pretty well. It's a nice change from the usual — you know, the ex-wife chasing down the ex-husband just to get support payments."

"Still, it'd be worth asking Amanda Blake a few more questions."

I'll say.

For a few moments there was complete silence from inside the house. Then, "Blake had been dead approximately six hours by the time Chloe and that boy found him. Amanda Blake told me she was home with her daughter all of the Saturday night and all of Sunday morning."

"That's pretty hard to verify," Steve said.

I thought about what Jessie had told me when I'd dropped by after her father died.

"Let's talk to the neighbours," Levesque said. "Find out if anyone saw her car leaving or returning to the house in that time frame." Another pause. "As I recall, she's not left-handed."

But David Mitchell was. So was at least one other person I could think of. Matt Solnicki. Did Levesque know that?

"She's also a small woman," Steve said. "Matt Solnicki, though, he's big. Suppose he suspected or found out that it was Blake who forced him off the road?"

What if that's what had happened? What if Matt

Solnicki had found out, and what if he'd decided to do something about it? I didn't want it to be true. It was bad enough that someone had murdered Jessie's dad. It was terrible to think that he might have been killed over something as stupid as a golf course. But at least if David Mitchell were the killer, Jessie wouldn't be hurt any more than she already had been. David Mitchell was a stranger to her. Matt Solnicki was someone she knew. Someone she liked. If he were the killer, Jessie would go from maybe having two fathers to having no father at all.

"First thing tomorrow I'll go and talk to them both," Levesque said. More silence. "Blake was killed where Chloe and that boy found him. We walked in there, Steve. I saw Chloe's footwear impressions. I saw the boy's. I saw yours and mine after we had documented the scene."

Well, of course he had. Hadn't he — or maybe it was Steve — said that the ground around there was soft?

"What I *didn't* see was Blake's footwear impressions, though." Oh. "Or the killer's. What do you make of that?"

Apparently Steve didn't make much of it because there was more silence, followed by what sounded like a sigh.

"Good work on those prints, Steve. I'm going to take another look at our budget, see if we can't send you on a few more courses. They're worth the money." He paused. "First thing tomorrow, I want you to go back out to the park and see if you can find anything, anything at all, that puts David Mitchell's vehicle on that road early Sunday morning."

"It's a busy road," Steve said.

"And Steve? Don't worry about Nelson. He won't be here forever." Steve must have nodded because the next thing Levesque said was, "I'll see you out."

I scrambled around to the front of the house and up onto the porch, dropped into my chair, picked up my book, opened it, and pretended to engross myself in it — all before the front door opened and Steve and Levesque stepped outside. Steve nodded a goodbye at me. Levesque stood at the top of the porch steps and watched him walk to his car and drive away. He turned and looked at me.

"Is that the book David Mitchell gave you?"

I nodded.

"Is it a good book?"

"Pretty good."

"You always read that way?"

I felt the heat rise in my cheeks. I glanced down to see if I'd done something stupid, like pick up the book and start to read it upside down. But no, it was right side up. Everything was fine — except for the guilty look on my face.

"What way?" I said.

"From back to front," Levesque said.

I gave him a genuinely baffled look.

"You left it open on the table inside," he said. "You were a lot farther along in it then than you are now."

Cops.

He stared up at the sky. "Nice bright night. Bright moon too. In the city, you don't notice what a difference a clear night and a bright moon makes. Up here, though, it's different, huh?"

Geez, what now?

"A bright moon like that casts shadows, just like the sun."

Oh boy.

He looked down at me now.

"When I ask you to leave Steve and me alone, that's what I expect you to do, Chloe."

He hadn't actually asked me to leave them alone. His exact words had been: Run along. But I didn't exactly have the moral high ground . . .

"You knew I was listening the whole time?"

The look he gave me would have soured milk.

"I trusted you to give us some privacy. If I'd known you were listening the whole time, you wouldn't have been listening. Understand?"

"I'm sorry." I was, too. Sorry that he'd caught me. Sorry that he seemed so disappointed in me. "It's just that . . . Well, I know the people involved."

"That's no excuse."

"I said I was sorry." Then, "The two guys who said they saw David Mitchell near where Trevor Blake was murdered — they seem to know Bryce Fuller pretty well."

Levesque looked at me.

"When I went looking for Adam a couple of days ago, those guys were at the Fuller place. Maurice

Dumont and Lyle Turnbull. They seemed pretty friendly with Adam's father."

"I know," Levesque said.

Oh. Well, maybe Mr. Super-Cop didn't know *this*: "Matt Solnicki is left-handed," I said.

No reaction. Well, if he was going to play cagey, I still had a thing or two to tell him.

"Jessie told me that she woke up sometime on Saturday night or early Sunday morning and her mother wasn't in the house. She says when she asked her mother where she'd been, Mrs. Blake said Jessie must have just dreamed she wasn't there. But Jessie told me it seemed so real. You don't think Mrs. Blake had anything to do with it, do you?"

He didn't say a word.

"And," I said, "a couple of days before that, Matt Solnicki proposed to Mrs. Blake."

For the first time in a very long time, I saw a look of surprise on Levesque's face.

chapter 14

I was up early because Mrs. Blake wanted me at her place first thing. Levesque was up even earlier and was pouring himself a cup of coffee when I walked into the kitchen.

"I don't know if it's a good idea for you to go out there," he said, "under the circumstances."

"What about Jessie?"

"You know I have to speak to Amanda Blake again."

"I promised Jessie that you'd find out who killed her father. If it turns out to be Matt Solnicki . . . " If it turned out her mother was in any way involved . . . I couldn't make myself say that, much less believe it. "I want to be with her," I said. "It's the right thing to do."

Levesque was silent for a few moments. Finally he nodded. "But you can't talk about the case. Not a word, not to anyone, not under any circumstances. You got it?"

"I got it," I said.

I was scurrying, gathering everything I planned to take with me, when I heard something strange outside. It sounded like . . . I went outside and looked up. It was. A helicopter. I went back inside to ask Levesque about it, but he was on the phone. I heard him ask a few questions — When? Where? How many? Who? His expression got grimmer and grimmer as he listened. When he hung up, he dumped his coffee into the sink and headed for the door.

"Problem?"

"The highway is barricaded."

"The *highway?*"

"It seems that the golf course protesters feel that David Mitchell is being framed for murder. They're trying to stop him from being transported to court."

"I just saw an OPP helicopter."

"They want to use it to transport him," Levesque said. "But if they do, there's going to be trouble for sure. Things have really escalated."

Escalated. I remembered what my mother had asked me: Are they armed? When people with guns, like the protesters, were facing other people with guns, like the OPP, and one side or the other escalated things, well, it was hard to see how anything positive could result.

"Be careful," I said.

He looked at me. "Sometimes — not very often, but sometimes — you sound exactly like your mother."

* * *

Mrs. Blake was waiting for me on her porch.

"I have appointments all day," she said. She looked coolly professional in a crisp summer suit, but her face was pale and there were dark circles under her eyes. "Fletcher is going to pick Jessie up around one and she's going to spend the rest of the day with him. She seems to have gotten even more attached to him since her father — " She broke off. Her eyes glistened and she swallowed hard. "I'd better run," she said. "Jessie is inside, looking at pictures. Maybe if you could get her out of the house for a while ..."

I said I'd see what I could do. I said maybe she'd want to go to the beach.

I found Jessie on the couch in the living room, leafing through a fat photograph album. Another stack of loose photos sat on the cushion beside her.

"Hey, Jessie," I said. "Can I look at those with you?"

She nodded without looking up from the album. I watched as she turned the pages slowly. Most of the pictures were of Trevor Blake, but Jessie was in some of them too. They seemed to be on vacation somewhere — wait, there was the CN Tower. They were in Toronto. There was Jessie waving on the observation deck at the top of the tower. Her father was waving too. Then they were together at the zoo. At Canada's Wonderland. At Casa Loma. In front of Niagara Falls. Hitting all the attractions southern Ontario had to offer.

When she finished the album, she set it aside and reached for the loose pictures. The ones one top were also of her father — at the beach, in the woods, by a boardwalk.

"The spruce bog, right?" I said. I remembered Jessie telling her uncle how much she liked that place.

Jessie nodded. "Daddy likes birds. We collected them at the bog."

"Collected them?"

"All the different kinds," she said. "We wrote down their names and tried to take pictures of them. Daddy made a book out of them. It's at his house."

Trevor Blake had been a bird watcher. Well, what do you know?

She reached for some more photos. "Uncle Fletcher took these," she said. They were recent pictures of Jessie and her father.

"At the amusement park up in Morrisville?" I said. She nodded. She flipped to pictures of herself, of her mother, of Jessie and her mother together. Nice close-up pictures, each one looking like a magazine layout.

"Your uncle sure is a good photographer," I said as I worked my way through the stack. There were a couple of pictures of Jessie, sitting on her uncle's knee.

"Did your mother take these?" I said.

"Uncle Fletcher took them. He has a thing that lets him take pictures of himself."

Some kind of remote attachment, I thought. There were also some nature shots and landscapes.

"What about these? Did you take them, Jessie?"

She shook her head. "Uncle Fletcher did. I printed them on the photo printer he gave me."

Was it just me, or was Fletcher Blake less accomplished with inanimate objects than he was with people? Not likely for someone who got published in *Canadian Geographic*. But some of these landscapes didn't seem to be of the same high quality as the people shots. For example, there was one park

177

landscape that showed grass and trees and shrubs, with red flowers — it looked like maybe sheep's laurel — in the background and, here and there, little swatches of yellow. That didn't seem to be nearly as carefully composed as one might expect from a famous photographer. I understood why Jessie had printed it, but I didn't understand why Fletcher Blake had taken it. Then I remembered what he had said to Mrs. Blake — that he liked to use a digital camera because it allowed him to take dozens, even hundreds, of photos, not all of which he used. Many he never even printed.

Jessie stared down at the picture. Tears welled up in her eyes.

"They found out who did it," she said. "Mom says he's locked up now and the police are taking him away. He's going to prison, right, Chloe? He's going to prison for the rest of his life."

I looked into her ten-year-old eyes. They were hard and fierce and filled with hate. I couldn't blame her. In her place, I would probably feel the same way. Levesque hadn't talked to Mrs. Blake yet. He hadn't asked her all the new questions he had. He hadn't told her what he had found out about the night Matt Solnicki and I were run off the road. What would happen when he did? How would Jessie feel then?

"Whoever did it is going to pay, Jessie," I said. That much I knew was true. The question was, how much more grief would Jessie have to endure before that payment was collected? "Hey,

Jessie, you want to go to the beach?"

She shook her head.

"You want to see if Megan can come over?"

Another shake of her head.

"You want to make cookies?" Baking was one of my secret baby-sitting weapons. So far I hadn't encountered a kid who wasn't interested in making cookies and then eating them when they were still warm.

"Uncle Fletcher likes chocolate chip cookies," she said. "With pecans, not walnuts."

"Then why don't we make some? You can give them to him when he comes to pick you up."

She nodded.

"But we should tidy up here first, okay?"

Jessie nodded and tucked the photo she had been holding into the album. While she took it upstairs to her room, I straightened up the loose photos and stacked them on the coffee table. Then we went into the kitchen, found a recipe and did an ingredient check. "We have everything we need," I said, "except pecans. Do you think it would be okay if we left those out?"

She did not. Not even remotely.

"It's okay," I said quickly. "Hey, Jessie, it's okay. We'll walk into town and buy some. It won't take long. We have plenty of time."

We walked into town, bought pecans and were strolling along Centre Street on our way back to Jessie's when Ross exploded out of the *Beacon* office. He did not look happy.

"Hey, Ross," I said mildly.

He scowled at me.

"You'll never guess what happened," he said. Then he looked at Jessie and said, "Never mind." The expression on his face screamed everything but 'never mind'. And he was my friend. So . . .

"Jessie, you think you could do something for me?" I said. "You think you could go into the drugstore and buy me some gum?" I fished some money out of my pocket. "Peppermint. And a pack for you too. I'll wait for you here, okay?"

She nodded and ran up the block to the store.

I turned to Ross. "What's up?"

"Fletcher Blake called Mr. Torelli yesterday — and Mr. Torelli just told me this morning."

"Told you what?"

"My audiotape, the one that Mr. Torelli gave to Fletcher Blake so that he could make a copy? It got destroyed."

"*Got* destroyed? You mean, Blake destroyed it?"

"Mr. Torelli said that Fletcher Blake sounded really embarrassed. He told Mr. Torelli that he felt like an idiot — I mean, he can handle all kinds of camera equipment and computers and is a whiz when it comes to digital technology. But old-fashioned audiotapes? Well, gosh, they just seem to defeat him. He said he was trying to make a copy of my tape and something went wrong and the tape was destroyed. *Something went wrong.* What does that even mean? What could possibly go wrong?"

"Calm down, Ross."

"It was my only source."

"I thought you were going to write down everything you could remember."

"Right," he said. He pulled a notebook from his back pocket and thrust it at me. "This is what I wrote. Look at it." I had barely opened the notebook, let alone started to read, when he said, "What do you notice?"

"That if they still taught penmanship as a separate subject in school, you'd fail?"

Ross rolled his eyes. "No quotes," he said. He practically screamed the words at me. "I remember some of what he said, but I don't have a single direct quote. How can you write a profile of someone without including even one single quote?"

I thought he was going to blow an artery or something. "You could always ask him for a second interview," I said. "After all, he's the one who wrecked your tape."

"You think I didn't think of that?"

"He said no, huh?"

"He's leaving town in a day or two. In the meantime, well, his brother just died." There was no trace of sympathy in Ross's voice.

"His brother *was* murdered, Ross."

"Whatever. I don't get my interview."

Jessie came out of the store, carrying a small bag. Ross turned and walked away.

"Your notes!" I called.

"They're garbage," he said, without turning back.

I stuffed the notebook into my purse, and Jessie and I headed home to make cookies.

* * *

Fletcher Blake's van was parked in the driveway when Jessie and I got back from town. He wasn't in it.

"He's probably in the house," Jessie said. "Mom gave him a key, just in case. Let's go surprise him."

We crept up onto the porch. Jessie tried the door. It was unlocked. She grinned at me. She pushed it open and snuck into the front hall.

Fletcher Blake was in the living room. He had Jessie's stack of photos on his lap and he was thumbing quickly through them.

"Surprise!" Jessie yelled.

Fletcher Blake started. The photos slid to the floor as he turned his wheelchair, a stunned look on his face. As soon as he saw it was Jessie, he relaxed and broke into a broad smile.

"I'm going to have to get you for that," he said.

Jessie giggled.

"You're early," she said. "We were going to surprise you."

"You *did* surprise me," he pointed out.

"No. I mean with cookies. We were going to make you cookies."

"Yum," Fletcher Blake said. "How about if I help you?"

Jessie shrieked her approval.

"Help me pick these up first," Fletcher Blake

said. Jessie bent to gather the photos. She froze when she saw the one on top — a close-up of her father. Gently her uncle pulled it from her. "Come on," he said. "Let's make those cookies."

. We went into the kitchen. Fletcher Blake put on some music and clowned around with us while we mixed the cookie dough. While we worked, he snapped pictures of us. It seemed as if he was always taking pictures.

After the cookies had cooled, we put them in a tin.

"I guess I better be going," I said.

"Why don't you change your T-shirt, Jessie, and we'll go to the movies?" Fletcher Blake said.

Jessie looked down at her T-shirt. It was dusted with flour and smudged with chocolate. "Okay," she said.

After she'd run upstairs he turned to me. "I hope it doesn't take long to get this case to trial," he said. "The sooner it's over, the sooner Jessie and Amanda can start to heal."

I nodded.

"I caught some buzz when I was in town earlier," he said. "About your father. Apparently he and that staff sergeant from the OPP had words. People are saying that your father doesn't see eye to eye with the OPP. They say he has doubts about this David Mitchell fellow. Is that true?"

"He likes to be thorough," I said.

"Are you saying that the OPP aren't thorough? There were eyewitnesses. They would hardly have arrested the man if they weren't sure he did it, would they?"

Jessie's feet thundered down the stairs.

"I'd better get my stuff together," I said. I went into the other room to pack up. As I did, I heard Fletcher Blake say, "You remember that picture you printed before we went to Toronto? Do you still have it, Jessie?"

"Why?" Jessie said.

"It's not a very good picture. I have better ones. I don't want you to remember me by a bad picture."

"I don't have it anymore," Jessie said. "I threw it away."

"Oh? So you didn't approve of the quality either?"

"I threw it away because it reminded me of Daddy."

In fact, she had done just the opposite. I wondered why she was lying to her uncle.

* * *

After I left Mrs. Blake's house, I went up to the beach to see if Adam was there. He wasn't. I called his cell. No service. I stopped at his house. No one was there either, so I decided to leave him a note. I rooted around in my bag for a pen. Found one. Now something to write on. The only thing I could find was Ross's notebook. I pulled it out, thumbed to the back for a blank page to write on, scrawled a note to Adam and slipped it under the door.

* * *

I was on my way home when my phone rang. I scrabbled around in my purse for it.

"Adam?" I said breathlessly.

"No," a deep voice said. "It's me."

Levesque.

"I won't be home tonight," he said.

"Why not?"

"Things are . . . " He paused. "They're a little tense."

"Did they take David Mitchell out by helicopter?"

"No."

"I heard you and Staff Sergeant Nelson got into some kind of argument."

"We had a difference of opinion." He sounded irritated, maybe by the argument or maybe because people were talking about it. "Do me a favour? Don't try to come out here. Stay in town."

I said I would. "I'm at Mrs. Blake's tomorrow," I said. "In case you need me for anything."

"Chloe? If your mother calls — "

"Don't tell her anything?"

"Tell her she can try me on my cell phone."

* * *

I fed Shendor and then myself. Mom called. She said East Hastings had made the news in Montreal and wanted to know if everything was okay. "So far, so good," I said, and passed along Levesque's message. I hoped nobody was shooting at anybody else when Mom got through to him. And then, because I didn't think I could stand the quiet anymore, I called Ross.

"I'm covering a softball game," he said. "But I could meet you later at Stella's."

"Done," I said.

I rode into town and parked myself at the counter at Stella's, where they still didn't serve latte or cappuccino. The softball game must have gone into extra innings because Ross wasn't there. He was still MIA fifteen minutes later when Roxie, the waitress, asked me if I wanted a refill. She stared at my chin while she poured me a fresh cup. After she left, I touched the spot she had been looking at. Was that what I thought it was? I touched it again. It felt like . . . I rummaged in my purse, found a mirror and peered into it. Yup, the beginning of a zit. It wasn't big yet, thank goodness. But with my luck, it would be visible from a kilometre away the next time I saw Adam.

When I tucked the mirror back into my purse, I felt something. Ross's notebook. I pulled it out. Poor Ross, he always aimed for the top in anything he did. So when he had scored an interview with "someone famous," as he put it, he had probably imagined a full-page story, complete with a photo. Or maybe *photos* because, after all, he was profiling a photographer. I flipped through his notebook. Ross had filled page after page with scribbly, scratchy writing: everything he remembered about his interview with Fletcher Blake.

Some of it looked pretty interesting. Places he remembered that Fletcher Blake had photographed — locations all over the country, from west coast to east coast to the far north. He had travelled the world, too, almost always with an assistant who helped him navigate some of the trickier terrain. He had been to some of the world's most environmentally sensitive places, and he'd talked to Ross about how he felt about what he was doing. How he worried that if he took pictures that captured the exquisite beauty of some of the places he had visited, it might prompt people to want to visit them, and that there was nothing more certain to ruin an environmentally sensitive place than mobs of tourists. He'd talked about how he was always careful to put everything back exactly the way he had found it, but that he'd been to places where other people hadn't even tried to be careful — pop cans in the wilderness, Ross had written, cigarette butts floating in ponds, plastic bags caught in treetops. I knew the feeling. I'm a city girl who has learned to love the country, and I get angry every time I come across candy wrappers and empty cigarette packs in East Hastings Provincial Park. It's as if people never bother to read the signs that are posted along the trails.

"Hey," a voice said. Ross slid onto the stool next to mine.

"Hey," I said. "You feeling better now?"

He shrugged.

I handed him his notebook. "There's some interesting stuff in here. It would make a great article, Ross."

"He spent hours with me. He showed me his whole set-up. He does everything digitally. You can't believe how clear his photos are, even when he super-enlarges them."

"Yes, I can," I said. "I saw some pictures he took of Jessie and her mom."

"He really gets the technology. He does these amazing composites. And he took some pictures of me."

"He did? You never showed me."

"That's because my mother saw them first. She loves them. Says they're the best pictures of me she's ever seen. And you know what? It wasn't like he was even concentrating on taking them. It's just something he does, the way some people doodle. He's always taking pictures. He says — "

" — you never know when you're going to catch something by chance. I know. I read your notes."

He sighed. "He's such an interesting guy. It really would have been a terrific article."

"So why don't you talk to him one more time before he leaves town? You've already done a face-to-face interview. You've seen all his stuff and how he works. Maybe he'll agree to a phone interview once he gets wherever he's going. That way you can get the quotes you're missing."

"I don't know," Ross said. "He's a busy man."

"He's also the person who mangled your tape. Maybe if you kind of hint at that, you know, make him feel a little guilty, maybe he'll say yes. You can't give up, Ross. You spent a lot of time on this. And there's good stuff in here."

"Maybe," Ross said. He didn't sound convinced.

He ordered a Coke and we sat there for a while, talking about what was happening out at the barricade and what might happen if the blockaders didn't back down. "I think your dad got through to them. Mr Torelli said he heard him remind the head OPP guy about what happened at Ipperwash." Ipperwash Provincial Park, he meant. Where the OPP had shot and killed a native protester named Dudley George.

chapter 15

When I woke up, Shendor was lying across the bottom of my bed, which told me that, true to what he had said, Levesque hadn't come home. I went outside and collected the *Beacon*. According to the lead story, there were more native activists on their way to East Hastings to support the blockaders. There were reports, unconfirmed, that police reinforcements would arrive today to deal with any "trouble" that might arise when David Mitchell was helicoptered out of town. And another report, also unconfirmed, that he would be transported today. The local Member of Parliament was quoted as saying that the police would be prudent to continue to negotiate with the protesters until some sort of compromise was reached. This, the MP said, would avoid any "unnecessary" bloodshed. I wondered what he would consider to be "necessary" bloodshed.

I made coffee, let Shendor out, let her back in again, and filled her bowl with food. Then I dressed and left for Mrs. Blake's house.

"I should be back by noon," Mrs. Blake told me. "I have to meet some new tenants. They weren't going to come at first — after what they heard on the news, they didn't think they'd be able to get through. But you can make the trip on side roads if you know the way — which they don't, but I do. So I have to be their navigator." She sighed. "I hope they clear up this blockade soon." She probably also wished that they would clear up the matter of her ex-husband's murder, but she didn't say that. She never said anything about him, I think because she was trying to avoid upsetting Jessie.

She was back a little sooner than she expected. She poured herself a glass of ice water from the fridge, drank it down and said, "You can't believe how hot it is out there. And the Dillers — the new tenants — they were so nervous about armed protesters and the blockade that I thought they were going to back out before they even got to the cottage. I wanted to make sure they stayed, so I helped them unpack and get settled — fast — so that they could get into the water, have a swim and cool down. Once they did that, they seemed to forget about driving back to Toronto. But, boy, I wanted to jump into the water with them." She flashed me a smile. She seemed relieved to be home.

The phone rang.

Mrs. Blake answered. While she listened to whoever was on the other end of the line, her smile drained away. "I have to go back into town," she said when she hung up. "Can you take Jessie over to Trev— to Jessie's father's place? Fletcher is there. He's leaving tomorrow, and I promised to help him pack up and load his van. Maybe you and Jessie could give him a hand. I'll get there as soon as I can."

After lunch, Jessie and I walked over to her

father's house. I glanced at her as we made our way up the gravel driveway. She walked slowly toward the wood-frame house and hesitated when she reached the front porch. Like Mrs. Blake's house, it was also fitted with a ramp, making it wheelchair accessible. I guessed that Fletcher Blake was a frequent visitor.

Jessie turned and looked at me. Her eyes glistened with tears. "I miss him," she said.

"I know."

Then she squared her small shoulders and marched up the steps.

"Uncle Fletcher!" she called. She opened the front door without knocking.

"In here," Fletcher Blake said.

We found him in a sunny, spacious room that looked out over the back of the property. Besides bedroom furniture, it contained computer equipment and stacks of plastic bins that Fletcher Blake was filling and organizing. He looked a little embarrassed when he saw me.

"Some people travel light," he said. "But I haven't quite mastered the art. After nearly two months on the road, I've accumulated a lot of stuff."

He looked over my shoulder toward the door and frowned.

"Where's your mother, Jessie?"

"She had to go into town. She said we should help you."

"Well, I can always use help from my favourite niece." He looked apologetically at me. "But you don't have to stay, Chloe. Jessie can give me a hand until Amanda gets here."

"I don't mind," I said. I really didn't. "Besides, I'm already here. Just tell us what needs to be done and we'll take care of it, right, Jessie?"

"Right," Jessie said.

He seemed to hesitate.

"Really, it's no problem, Mr. Blake." I glanced around. "I can carry some of this stuff out to your van if you want."

"I'm not quite ready for that yet. But I do want to leave everything spic and span." Just like he left nature, I thought. "Jessie, there's a bunch of photography magazines in the living room. How about bringing them in here so that I can pack them? And the place could use a once-over with the vacuum cleaner. And the fridge should probably be cleaned out. And . . . " He looked at me. "Listen to me. I sound like the Wicked Stepmother giving orders to a couple of Cinderellas."

"We don't mind, do we, Jessie?" I said. She shook her head.

"Can I vacuum?" Jessie said.

I looked at Fletcher Blake, who smiled at me and shrugged.

"I'll get the vacuum cleaner for you," I said. "Do you know where your fa— " I broke off, annoyed at myself. I had almost come right out and said 'father.' I glanced at Jessie. She hadn't reacted.

"It's in the closet at the back of the house," Fletcher Blake said.

Annoyed with myself and vowing to be more careful, I went to get it. I set it up for her, and while she vacuumed I carried stacks of photography magazines into the back room where Fletcher Blake put them into a bin. When he had finished, he said, "That can go out to the van. The back is open. And this can go too." He dropped a folded tarp onto the top of the bin.

I carried the bin outside and swung it up into the van. Boy, I had never seen a vehicle as spotless as Fletcher Blake's van. A set of sturdy black cases had been fastened in place along one side of the interior to hold equipment and supplies. In front of the cases, on the floor, was an assortment of what looked like gardening equipment — a couple of rakes, a small shovel, a push broom. Okay, so the push broom wasn't gardening equipment. Clipped to the wall of the van was a detachable portable vacuum cleaner. Fletcher Blake obviously took neatness to the extreme. Not only was he determined to leave his brother's house as spotless as he apparently left his photography locations, but he also kept his personal possessions in pristine condition. Besides the equipment, there were also a couple of folded tarps, similar to the one he had dropped onto the bin of magazines. I slid the bin as far in as I could get it, so that there would be plenty of room for whatever he wanted to load next.

He was busy sorting through photos and digital photographic equipment when I went back inside. Jessie had abandoned the vacuum cleaner and was sitting on his knee, "helping" him.

"I'm going to start on the kitchen," I said.

I don't even know if they heard me. Half an hour later, I was hauling a green garbage bag out to the trash cans at the back of the house when, *oh boy*. There were three cans. Two of them had been tipped over and their contents strewn on the ground. Raccoons, I guessed. Not likely to be stopped by the lid of a garbage can. I was surprised that the lids hadn't been better secured. But maybe that was just since Trevor Blake had died. Maybe Fletcher Blake wasn't aware of the raccoon problem.

I went back into the kitchen and opened the cupboard under the sink to grab a box of green garbage bags. I also found a pair of rubber kitchen gloves. They were yellow, just like the ones Ed Winslow had found out at his place. I pulled on the gloves and went back outside to clean up the mess the raccoons had made, making sure to breathe through my mouth. Yuck, what a mess. I tried not to look at the glop that I was shovelling into the garbage bags. But you know how it is. Sometimes the harder you try not to look, the more likely you are to see.

I saw something.

Seeing something in a heap of garbagey goo and reaching into that garbagey goo to pick up that something are two different things, so for sure I wouldn't have bothered if it weren't for the handwriting. Scribbly, scratchy handwriting that was, as

I had already discovered, quite decipherable. It was Ross's handwriting, on one of those thin little stick-on labels that come with audiocassettes so that you can keep track of what's been recorded on the tape.

According to the label, it was Ross's interview with Fletcher Blake.

It was the cassette that had somehow been destroyed.

Except that it didn't look even remotely destroyed. There was no tape spilling out of it. The case didn't look broken. It wasn't even particularly gooey or gloppy. In fact, apart from its surroundings, it looked perfectly fine.

I picked it up and wiped it off.

"What do you have there?" said a voice behind me, startling me. I spun around. Fletcher Blake was gliding down the path toward me in his wheel-chair, a bag of trash on his lap.

"Raccoons got into the cans and made a real mess," I said. "I was just cleaning it up."

He looked at the audiocassette I was holding. Then he looked at me and sort of shrugged. He seemed embarrassed. "I see you found my deep, dark secret," he said. "Your friend from the local newspaper interviewed me."

My friend? How did he know — ?

"That boy I saw you with at the funeral," he said. "Nice kid. Eager. He did a long interview with me. Did a good job too. But when I listened to the tape, I sounded like a pompous know-it-all and, believe it or not, that's not the kind of person I am. So I threw it out and told the editor of the paper a little white lie. Your friend seems like a good kid. I hated to do it. But it seemed kinder to tell him the tape was ruined than to tell him I had flat-out changed my mind about being interviewed."

It may have seemed kinder to Fletcher Blake, but it hadn't come across that way to Ross. To him, it was just a bitterly missed opportunity.

"Fletcher? Fletcher?"

Mrs. Blake's voice, sounding — what? — excited? No, that wasn't it. More like upset.

Fletcher Blake swung his wheelchair around and called to her. Mrs. Blake appeared on the back porch, her face flushed.

"The police think Matt did it," she said. "They think Matt killed Trevor. And from the questions they were asking me — oh, Fletcher, I think they think I had something to do with it."

"*What?* Did they arrest Matt?"

"No, but the questions they asked him — " She broke off. Her eyes skipped to me and then darted back to Fletcher Blake. "Where's Jessie?" she said.

"Inside," Fletcher said. "I left her in the back room. She's vacuuming."

Mrs. Blake looked at me again. It wasn't hard to read what was in her eyes.

"I'll go inside and see how she's doing," I said. "I'll finish this later." I slipped the cassette into the box of garbage bags. I didn't know whether it was even playable and I was a little unclear about whether Ross could even use it without Fletcher Blake's permission, but I figured he deserved to know the whole story and to have his cassette back. I walked slowly back to the house, hoping Mrs. Blake would say something else, but she didn't. She was waiting until I was safely out of earshot.

I put the box of plastic garbage bags back where I had found it and slipped Ross's tape into my purse before I went into the bedroom. Jessie had finished vacuuming and was sitting on the bed, holding a camera and peering into the display screen.

"Shouldn't you ask permission before you do that?" I said.

She shook her head. "Uncle Fletcher always lets me see his pictures. Always."

"Anything interesting?"

She held the camera out to me. I saw a photo of Jessie on the display screen. She was holding an ice cream cone.

"I bet he took that yesterday," I said. "In Morrisville."

Jessie nodded. She wasn't smiling now and she wasn't smiling in the photograph.

I glanced out the window into the backyard. Mrs. Blake had gone down off the porch and was standing near her ex-brother-in-law, talking to him, her face creased with worry. He stared up at her, his expression sombre, and shook his head slowly. They started back toward the house, Mrs. Blake walking beside his wheelchair. Then he stopped and turned around. He sat there for a long time, motionless. Mrs. Blake approached him. She must have said something because he shook his head. They turned again. This time she followed him up the ramp into the house.

"Don't worry," he said as they came into the house.

"But if anything — "

"I'll call my agent," he said. "If necessary, I'll get her to push back that assignment so that I can stay for a few more days. Don't worry. We'll talk it through tonight, over dinner."

"But, Fletcher — "

"Don't worry, Amanda. It's going to be just fine."

"Fletcher, I don't know what I'd do if you weren't here. You always listen to me." Her voice was filled with gratitude. They came into the room where Jessie and I were.

"Come on, sweetie," Mrs. Blake said. "Let's go home. Chloe, can you baby-sit tonight?"

I wished I could have said I had plans — *Adam* plans — but I didn't. So I said, sure. And if Adam finally did call, well, he'd just have to learn to plan ahead.

"Can I drop you somewhere?" Mrs. Blake said.

I shook my head. "I'm okay. I'll see you tonight."

I walked to the car with them. Fletcher Blake followed. After Mrs. Blake and Jessie had driven away, Fletcher Blake said, "What did you do with that cassette?"

"I put it back where I found it," I said. "In the garbage. Do you want me to try to find it for you?"

I hoped that my expression conveyed two things: one, that I would look for it if he wanted me to, and two, that I hoped he wouldn't want me to, because the garbage was gross and smelly. He looked at me for a moment. "No," he said. "It's okay. But do me a favour? Don't mention to your friend that you found it. Okay?"

"No problem," I said. And it wasn't. Because I wasn't planning to *mention* the tape to Ross. I was planning to return it.

chapter 16

When I got home, I phoned Ross at work and ended up with his voicemail. I tried his house. His mother answered.

"He's out in the park," she said. "The nature centre has invited a scientist — oh dear, what was his name? Ross told me a dozen times." But she couldn't remember. "He's giving a talk on the park's ecology, and Ross is covering it for the *Beacon*."

Poor Ross. I knew he'd rather be at the barricade. I told his mother I'd catch up with him later.

I walked over to Mrs. Blake's that night, figuring I would get a drive home. Before I set out, I left a note to tell Levesque where I was. I thought about calling him, but he had left me a message on the phone at home saying that he was going to be tied up. He didn't say what he was doing, which meant that whatever it was, it was *official police business*. Maybe he was working on the situation at the blockade or maybe he was working on the Trevor Blake murder investigation. Whichever it was, I'd probably be the last person to find out.

"Jessie has already eaten," Mrs. Blake said. She looked sensational in a sleeveless blue summer dress that highlighted her sapphire eyes. "She can stay up until nine and then it's straight to bed, no arguments. Right, Jessie?"

Jessie nodded, but as soon as her mother's back

was turned, her eyes begged me for a little extra time. I winked at her.

I heard tires crunching up the gravel driveway, and Mrs. Blake said, "I'd better go. I don't want to make him get out. Jessie, do you want to come and say hi to your uncle?"

She sure did. She grabbed my hand and dragged me outside with her.

Fletcher Blake was sitting behind the wheel of his van. He rolled down the window and smiled at Mrs. Blake.

"Amanda, you look terrific. Doesn't she, Jessie?"

Jessie nodded. Fletcher Blake looked briefly at me. His smile seemed a little forced. Then he said, "I brought you something, Amanda." He handed down a small box. Mrs. Blake looked at it, frowning. Then she opened it.

"What's in it, Mom? What's in it?" Jessie said. She crowded her mother so that she could get a good look.

"Oh, Fletcher," Mrs. Blake said. She stared up at him. "I didn't know you still had this."

He seemed pleased by her reaction. "I was wondering if you would remember."

"How could I forget?" She held it out for Jessie to admire. It was a gold ring set with a blue stone that was an almost perfect match to Mrs. Blake's eyes. "Your Uncle Fletcher gave this to me, oh, way back when." She laughed.

"When we weren't really much more than kids," Fletcher Blake said. "When we — "

Mrs. Blake gave him a look.

"Well, let's just say it was a long time ago," he said. "Come on, Amanda. I made reservations. We don't want to be late."

Jessie begged to see the ring one more time. Then Mrs. Blake got into the van, and Jessie and I went back into the house.

Jessie wanted to watch a DVD, an Olsen Twins movie, for maybe the twentieth time since I had started baby-sitting her. I didn't understand the attraction, but I said, why not? Before she settled in, I asked if she had a Walkman.

"Mom has one," she said, hitting the pause button on the remote. "I can get it for you."

"Do you think she'd mind?"

Jessie was sure she wouldn't. She ran to fetch it. When she went back to her movie, I fished Ross's tape out of my bag. I cleaned it up as best I could with a couple of tissues and then dropped it into the Walkman. When I pressed Play, all I heard was humming and hissing. It looked as if the tape had been ruined by all the glop in the garbage after all. I was about to press the Stop button when I heard something. Fletcher Blake's voice. Followed by Ross's, asking a question. The tape faded in and out, but mostly it played reasonably well. No wonder Ross had been angry when he'd found out that it had been destroyed. It was a pretty good interview. Ross had asked good questions that proved that he'd done his homework. Ms Peters would have been proud. And he was right. The answers were fascinating — particularly Fletcher Blake's answer to Ross's question: "You say you make sure to leave things exactly the way you found them. How do you know they're *exactly* the same?" It made me wonder.

"Hey, Jessie?" I said after I'd finished listening to the tape. "You know that photograph album you showed me yesterday? The one with all of the pictures of your father?"

Her eyes came away from the screen.

"Do you mind if I see it again?"

"Okay," she said slowly. She paused the DVD.

"I'll get it," I said. "I don't want to interrupt your movie."

"It's in my room, on my bedside table."

I found the album and sat on Jessie's bed to flip through it. Near the middle I found what I was looking for — the landscape that Jessie had slipped in between the pages the other day. The photograph of her favourite place — the spruce bog. I looked at it again, at the sheep's laurel and at the little swatches of yellow. I peered more closely at them. Swatches of yellow, but not flowers. No. Bits of yellow plastic rope.

Someone sat down lightly on the bed beside me. Jessie. She took the picture from my hand.

"You told your uncle that you threw this one away," I said. "Why?"

"Because he doesn't like it. And when he takes pictures he doesn't like, he never keeps them. He either doesn't print them or, if he does print them

204

and he doesn't like them, he tears them up."

"Is that why you always look in his camera?"

She nodded. "Sometimes I like pictures that he doesn't."

"Like that one," I said.

She nodded.

"Will you let me borrow it?"

She slipped down off the bed, opened the drawer of her bedside table, and took out another photograph, a duplicate of the one in her hand.

"I printed two of them," she said. "I was going to give one to Daddy." Her voice trailed off. She handed the duplicate picture to me. "You can keep it," she said. "But don't let Uncle Fletcher see it. I don't want him to know I told a lie. But it was a white lie, right, Chloe?"

"Right," I said.

We went downstairs and I put the photo carefully in my purse.

"Can we go outside?" she said. "Can we have cookies and lemonade out there?"

"I have to make a phone call first," I said. "Why don't you go into the kitchen and get some cups — plastic ones — and put some cookies on a plate and I'll be there in a minute, okay?"

"Okay." She ran into the kitchen. I dug my cell phone out of my bag and dialled Levesque's number. He answered on the third ring.

"Are you all right?" he said, obviously knowing from his phone display that it was me.

"I'm fine. I'm baby-sitting at Mrs. Blake's. I — "

"So this isn't urgent?"

Urgent? "Well, I . . . "

"Then it's going to have to keep."

"Yeah, but — "

"It's going to have to keep," he said again, firmly. "I'll get back to you as soon as I can."

Call terminated.

I shoved the phone back into my bag and went to look for Jessie.

We sat in the doorway to the tent, eating cookies, drinking lemonade and looking up at the stars. Jessie was quiet except for munching.

"Are you okay, Jessie?"

"I heard Mom crying."

I didn't say anything.

"I heard her tell Matt she was afraid because of what the police said to him." She looked at me with wide, serious eyes. "What *did* the police say?"

"I don't know. Did you ask your mother?"

She nodded. "She said I must have heard wrong. Then she got mad at me for listening when she was having a private conversation with Matt. But how could it be private when she was talking so loud?"

I glanced at my watch. "It's ten-thirty," I said. "Past your bedtime. We'd better go inside."

It was even later by the time she had brushed her teeth and changed into her pyjamas, and I'd read her a story and then another one. Finally she let me shut off the light and close her door. I went downstairs and turned on the TV. At eleven-thirty I heard a car in the driveway. A few moments later, a key turned in the lock and Mrs. Blake came inside. She looked upset. Maybe she was still thinking about what had happened that afternoon. She said, "Fletcher will drive you home."

"It's okay," I said. She looked like she wanted someone — Fletcher — around to talk to. "I can find my own way."

"It's late. And dark. And things are so unsettled. Please, Chloe. I'd feel a lot better knowing that you weren't walking all the way home on your own." I agreed, but only because she insisted. Besides, I thought, it was a ten-minute drive. What could possibly happen? Then I remembered my ten-minute drive with Matt Solnicki. Plenty had happened that night.

Mrs. Blake walked me out and saw me safely into the front passenger seat. It was my first close-up view of the front interior of the van. I saw now that it was equipped with hand controls. Fletcher Blake put the van into reverse and then used a hand control to apply the gas. We were out of sight of Mrs. Blake's house when he stopped suddenly and said, "What was that?"

"What was what?"

"That bump. Did you feel it?"

"It's a gravel road," I said. "They're all a little bumpy."

He rolled down his window, looked out and then turned back to me, frowning. He reached toward me and, I don't know why exactly, I pulled back. He gave me a strange look, reached a little farther, opened the glove compartment and pulled out a flashlight.

"Can I ask you to do me a favour, Chloe? I know I felt something. Would you mind taking a look? I could do it myself, but it would take me a lot longer, and I know you want to get home." He held out the flashlight. "I'm sure I heard something under the driver's-side rear wheel," he said. "Or maybe it's the tire. I had it patched when I was down east, but I never got around to replacing it, which, for a guy in my situation, is pretty stupid. But no one's perfect, right?"

I took the flashlight from him. He smiled gratefully.

I opened the door, got out, circled around to the back of the van and shone the light under the rear wheel. I didn't see anything but gravel. The tire looked fine too. I checked the other wheel and wished I could just walk home from here. But I'd left my purse in the van. I climbed back inside.

"Everything looks fine," I said.

Fletcher Blake returned the flashlight to the glove compartment and thanked me.

"I was wondering about that tape," he said.

"What tape?" I had left my purse on the floor at my feet when I got out of the van. I glanced down. It was still there.

"The audiotape. The one you found in the garbage earlier today. You said you left it where you found it, didn't you?"

"Yes," I said. My hand went to the door handle.

"You really don't have to drive me, Mr. Blake. I can — "

"I got to thinking about what I had done, about how I hadn't been honest with that young reporter friend of yours. So I looked for it. But I couldn't find it. I don't suppose you know where it is, do you?"

"No," I said.

He looked at me for a few seconds before he said, "What about that picture?"

"What picture?"

"The one that was in your purse."

Was?

I felt numb all over. I forced myself to look directly at him and willed myself to keep calm — or, at least, to look calm. I reached down and picked up my purse.

"I'm going to walk home," I said. As my hand moved back to the door handle, all the locks in the van *tchonk*ed shut. I glanced at Fletcher Blake. His hand was on the driver's-side panel, on the button that controlled all of the windows and all of the locks.

"They're child-proofed," he said. "All of them. So no one gets hurt."

I was trapped.

"Mr. Blake," I said, my voice trembling, "I'd like to get out."

No response.

I groped in my purse for my cell phone. It was gone. So were the audiocassette and the photograph.

"Mrs. Blake knows I'm with you," I said.

"And I intend to let her know that I delivered you safely home."

He said it so nicely that part of me actually believed that everything was going to be okay. He was going to drive me home. When I got there, I could lock the door and call Levesque. Then I thought about the cell phone, the photo and the audiocassette that had been in my purse when I got into the van. All of those things were now gone. There might be a logical explanation for that. But the only one I could think of made me believe that everything was definitely *not* going to be okay.

"I'm curious about that photograph," Fletcher Blake said. "Where did you get it?"

"Jessie gave it to me."

"Really? She told me she'd thrown it out."

"She likes it. It reminds her of her father. She thought if she gave it to you, you'd destroy it."

"And yet she gave it to you. Why is that?"

"I like it too."

"Do you?" His tone made it clear that he didn't believe me. "Does it speak to you?"

"I beg your pardon?"

"The photo. Does it speak to you? Do you see something in it that perhaps other people don't? That's what draws people to certain images — they see something in them, or imagine that they see something."

I said nothing.

"Perhaps you were planning to give it to your father."

"I wasn't planning anything," I said. "Look, Mr. Blake — "

He pulled the photo from a storage compartment between the two front seats and looked at it for a moment. Then he reached for me — no, across me again, to the glove compartment. He popped it open and thrust a hand inside. I held my breath until I saw that what he pulled out was *not* a gun. It wasn't a weapon at all, unless the crime he had in mind was arson. He was holding a book of matches. He lit a match, touched it to the corner of the photo, then, *whrrr*, down went the driver's-side window. He held the photo out the van window until it was all but consumed by flame. Then he dropped it to the gravel below.

"It really wasn't a very good photograph," he said.

"I'd like to get out now, Mr. Blake."

"I'm afraid that's not possible."

I scrabbled for the door lock and tried to pry it up. It wouldn't give. He produced a length of yellow cord from under his seat, and for some reason that scared me more than if he had pulled out a gun.

"I'm sorry," he said.

Sorry?

He grabbed my left wrist and wrenched it so that I had no choice but to twist in my seat, giving him an even better grip. I cried out in pain.

"Now the other one," he said. "Put your other hand behind your back."

No way, I thought. If I did that, I wouldn't have a

chance. He had a tight grip on my left wrist, but I still had my purse in my other hand, and I swung it, hitting him in the face with it as hard as I could. He cursed, wrenched it from my hand and shoved me hard into the passenger door. I put out my right hand to try to lessen the impact. Then, boy, I felt pain, like a flash of light: bright, hot, searing. And what was that sound, like something cracking? My arm throbbed and burned, and tears welled up in my eyes.

"I'm going to ask you one more time," he said.

He grabbed my damaged — broken? — arm and pulled it behind my back. I whimpered in pain as he tied my hands together.

"I'm sorry," he said again as he started the engine. My arm felt like it was on fire. For a few moments, it was all I could think about — that maybe it was broken, and that, if it was, maybe being wrenched behind my back like that would cause permanent damage. I tried to remember what I had learned in first aid about broken bones and what could go wrong — as if things could possibly get worse than they already were.

I glanced at Fletcher Blake. Both of his hands were square on the steering wheel. I hadn't paid them much attention before, but I sure did now. They were big hands. Strong hands. His arms were strong too. His muscles bulged. I tried to remember if he was left-handed.

"I have a mother," I said. "And two sisters, one younger, one older."

In other words, I was someone. A real person, with a real family who would miss me if anything happened to me.

"Do you look up to your older sister?"

The question took me by surprise. He looked at me, waiting for an answer.

"I guess," I said. I *like* my older sister. If you pushed me, I'd even admit that I love her. After all, she's my sister. I've known her all my life. And at that exact moment, I would have done anything — absolutely anything — to see her again. Then, because he was Jessie's uncle, because I had seen them together, because I knew he loved her, and because that meant that somewhere inside there had to be something good in him, I said, "My arm — I think it's broken."

"I looked up to my big brother. I wanted to be just like him. He was smart. He was charming. He could build anything — absolutely anything. And athletic?" He shook his head. "He was on the football team in high school and in college. He was good too. And the girls? They lined up to go out with him."

I looked out the window. We were headed back to Trevor Blake's place.

"That's where Amanda met him, you know. At college."

I looked at my purse and wondered what he had done with my phone.

"You know how people say that some girls are so pretty that they turn heads?"

x

213

My arms were tightly tied behind my back. I felt sick from the pain. But maybe when he stopped the van and opened the door . . . I could hardly breathe when I thought about it . . . maybe before he took me into the woods or wherever he was planning to take me . . .

"That's the way it was with Amanda," he said. "She'd walk across campus and every head would turn to look at her. Every head. Trevor's. Mine."

He flipped on the turn signal. We were on a deserted road, headed for who knew where, and he flipped on the turn signal. Old habits die hard.

He parked the van behind his brother's house and opened the driver's-side door. Maybe after he got out, I could . . .

He turned, looked at me and shook his head.

"You didn't do up your seat belt," he said. I cried out as he forced me back in the seat, back against my sore arm, and fastened the belt for me. "There. That will keep you safe and sound." He groped in the back of the van for something. A rag, neatly folded. He scrunched it up, then reached across me and pinched my nose shut. As soon as I opened my mouth, he jammed the rag inside. At first I thought he was going to suffocate me. Then he let go of my nose. He leaned back in his seat and stared out the window for a moment. Then he pulled a cell phone — my cell phone — from the pocket of the driver's-side door.

He pressed a button to activate the car seat. It swivelled so that his back was to me, and then lowered him to the ground. Another button activated the van's side door and lowered his wheelchair for him. I struggled against the seat belt, tears of pain and frustration rolling down my cheeks. A few moments later, the passenger door opened and Fletcher Blake reached for my purse. He opened it, dropped my cell phone inside and tucked the purse behind him. Then he reached over, released my seat belt, took hold of my sore arm and yanked me out of the van. It hurt so much that I thought I was going to faint. Then he dragged me with him toward the ramp that led up into the house. I tried, exactly once, to pull in the opposite direction, and got a sick feeling all over. My arm was definitely broken. I stumbled into the house beside him. A couple of times he yanked on my arm, maybe by accident, maybe on purpose. I felt like throwing up. Once we were inside, he stopped and looked around. I think he was trying to decide what to do with me. He tossed my purse onto the kitchen counter. Then he opened a utility cupboard and pulled out some more bright yellow plastic cord.

chapter 17

Fletcher Blake forced me into a closet at the back of the house. He pushed me against a pipe that came up through the closet floor and continued on up through the ceiling, tied me securely to it, bound my ankles and tied a clean dishtowel over my mouth to keep the gag in place.

"I need to think," he said. "I know that your mother is out of town and your father is out at the blockade. Something to do with that fellow they arrested for Trevor's murder."

I felt faint and numb all over.

"I don't have many options." He shook his head. "I need to think."

He backed his wheelchair out of the closet and closed the door. Now what?

He knew Levesque was still in town, so he must also have known that I'd be missed, probably sooner rather than later. Whatever he was going to do, he would have to do it soon. If he untied me again, maybe I'd have a chance. If he didn't . . . tears stung my eyes as I thought about the possibilities. I fought back the panic that gripped me. What was he doing out there? What options was he considering? Was surrender one of them?

After a while I heard a sound from somewhere outside. A faint crunching. A car, maybe, on the gravel driveway? Or my overactive imagination? Then I heard a bell. The doorbell? No, it couldn't be. Who would come calling so late? Who — I heard voices. A man's and a woman's. They got louder.

"I had to come," the woman was saying. It was Mrs. Blake. Mrs. Blake was out there, maybe even in the kitchen.

"Let's go to the other room," Fletcher Blake said. "We can talk there."

I pulled against my bindings. My arm protested. If I hadn't been gagged, my screams would have woken the dead.

"I couldn't leave things the way they were," Mrs. Blake said.

"What about Jessie?" Fletcher Blake said. "Is she home alone? Because if she is — "

"She's in the car," Mrs. Blake said. "She was awake when I got home, looking at pictures of Trevor."

"Amanda, it's late. And you look tired. You and Jessie could both use a good night's sleep. You should go home. We can talk in the morning."

"But that's just it, Fletcher. There's nothing to talk about."

"Amanda, there's so much going on right now. You shouldn't make any quick decisions. Trevor just died — "

"Trevor and I were divorced for five years." A slight pause. "Fletcher, I'm flattered that you asked me." Asked her what? "Really I am. But I'm going to marry Matt. I love him."

Oh. I thought back to what I had heard Fletcher Blake say the day that Jessie and I were in the tent. He'd said that he was one of the men she knew who had had bad luck. I thought about the ring he had given her tonight — the ring he had obviously given to her some time in the past. The ring that she had just as obviously given back to him.

"Amanda, it's late. You should go home and sleep on it."

"I don't need to sleep on it. I had to tell you, Fletcher," she said. "I didn't want to leave you with any false hopes."

Then: "Mom, I'm thirsty."

"Jessie, I asked you to wait in the car."

I pulled my ankles hard against the cord, trying to free them so that I could thump on the floor, anything to attract some attention.

"But I'm thirsty."

The cords were tied tightly.

I heard the tap run in the kitchen. "Here," Mrs. Blake said.

Silence for a moment. Then a small sound, a musical jingle. A cell phone ringer. My cell phone ringer. Then Jessie's voice again, high and clear: "What's Chloe's purse doing here?"

"Oh," her uncle said. "She left it in the car. I was going to return it to her tomorrow."

"Someone's calling her," Jessie said. "Maybe we should take her purse back to her, Mom."

"Jessie, it's late."

I twisted my ankles, trying to work the cord free. It refused to give. Then I started to grunt as loudly as I could, over and over until I thought my lungs would explode.

"What on earth is that?" Mrs. Blake said. "It sounds like it's coming . . . "

Footsteps came toward me. I kept grunting, like an enormous, crazed wild pig.

"Amanda . . . " Fletcher Blake's voice. He must have been right outside the door.

Then the door opened and light flooded the closet. Mrs. Blake gaped at me. Then she closed the door.

"Jessie, go and wait in the car."

"What is it?" Jessie said, her voice full of terror. "What's in there?"

"Go and wait in the car," Mrs. Blake said again. I had never heard her sound so stern.

Light footsteps faded into the distance. A door opened and closed. Then light flooded the closet again, and Mrs. Blake came in and removed the gag from my mouth. Her hands and fingers trembled as she bent and undid the cord securing my ankles. When she went to work on the one around my arms, I whimpered.

"My arm," I said weakly.

"I don't know what's going on here, Fletcher," Mrs. Blake said. "But I'm taking Chloe out of here and then I'm going to call her father." She was trying to sound calm, as if she were in control of the situation. But her fingers fumbled with the cord and when she bent closer so that she could see what she was doing, I saw that her expression was strained.

"Amanda," Fletcher Blake said. He positioned his chair in the entrance to the kitchen. "Please."

"He killed Mr. Blake," I said. "He killed your ex-husband."

Mrs. Blake acted as if she hadn't heard me. She finished undoing the cord around my arms. "Are you all right?" she said.

I nodded, even though my arm felt as though it had been doused with gasoline and set on fire.

"I'm taking you home," she said. She guided me to the door and waited there for Fletcher Blake to move his wheelchair back to let us pass.

But he didn't move.

"Amanda, please, let me explain."

"Let us out, Fletcher."

"Amanda, he had to be stopped."

She stared at him. If she was afraid, she gave no sign of it.

"He tried to kill Matt," Fletcher Blake said. "You know it and the police know it."

"They told me they're pretty sure it was Trevor," she said. "But they don't know why he would do something like that. And neither do I. It doesn't make any sense. He knew Matt. They even worked together on some jobs. Why would Trevor want to hurt him?"

"Because you were going to marry him," Fletcher Blake said.

Mrs. Blake stared at him for a moment. Then her head started to tick from side to side. No. No. No.

"Amanda, it wasn't the first time. Remember you told me about Jeff Ashby and Brian Meadows?"

Who? I didn't recognize the names.

"What are you saying, Fletcher?"

"Remember what you said? You said that the men you get involved with have bad luck? Jeff was in a car accident just like Matt, wasn't he? With Brian, it was a boating accident." Fletcher Blake reached out with one hand. "Amanda," he said, talking softly to her now, "don't you see?" She backed away from him. "It wasn't bad luck. It was Trevor. I don't know if anyone could prove it now that he's dead, but it was Trevor."

For a moment Mrs. Blake just stood there, silent. Her voice was weak when she said, "If you knew or suspected that Trevor had anything to do with Matt's accident — "

"It was no accident, Amanda."

" — you should have gone straight to the police."

"At first I couldn't believe it. He was my brother. But — " He shook his head. "The night Matt was run off the road, I was here. Trevor was out all day, working. I decided to start supper. There was some hamburger meat in the fridge, and you know how much Trev liked grilled burgers."

"Fletcher — "

"Please, Amanda, just let me explain."

It took a moment, but finally she nodded.

"He came home just as I was unwrapping the

meat. He grabbed it from me and said it was no good — it had spoiled and he'd meant to throw it out. He said he had some steaks in the fridge instead. So I took them outside and barbecued them. After we ate, Trevor said he had to go out to run some errands. While he was getting ready, I cleaned up. The hamburger meat was still in the fridge. I thought that was funny — he'd said he was going to throw it out. I don't know why I did it, but I checked the meat. It smelled fine. So I thought, okay, he just wasn't in the mood for burgers, but he didn't want to hurt my feelings. While he was out, I did some work — I was playing with some photos I'd taken. Around ten or so I went to the fridge to get a beer. The hamburger meat was gone."

My arm was throbbing. I felt woozy. I wanted to sit down before I fell down or passed out. But I forced myself to stand there and listen.

"Fletcher, please — "

"The funny thing is, even after I read in the paper about that dog being poisoned, it never even occurred to me that Trevor might have done it," Fletcher said. "I figured that what happened to Matt had something to do with that situation with the golf course. That's what everyone was saying. If I hadn't run into that friend of yours, that Lloyd fellow — "

"Derek?"

"I ran into him in town."

I remembered what Ross had said. He had seen Fletcher Blake and Derek Lloyd together at the gas station the day before Adam and I had found Trevor Blake's body in the bog.

"What does Derek have to do with this?"

"He looked embarrassed to see me. And nervous."

I remembered how nervous he had looked when he had first come to Mrs. Blake's house and thought that she was still married to Trevor. He'd relaxed when he heard about the divorce, but had tensed up again when he learned that Trevor Blake still lived nearby.

"Amanda, Trevor threatened him."

"*Threatened?* Nonsense. Trevor didn't even know he was in town."

"I don't mean recently. I mean before."

"Before?"

"Before you were married. When you were just starting to go out with Trevor and you were still seeing other people. Derek was one of those people, wasn't he?"

Mrs. Blake nodded. "You can't think that Trevor threatened — "

"I *know* he did, Amanda. Derek told me. Trevor told him to stay away from you . . . or else. He really scared him, Amanda. That's why Derek didn't rent a cottage here in East Hastings. That's why he went farther north. He didn't want to take the chance of running into Trevor again. He wouldn't even have stopped in town if he hadn't had car trouble. The whole time I was talking to him, he was nervous. Afraid Trevor might show up."

"Fletcher, you can't possibly think — "

"Amanda, listen. Trevor did it to me too."

She just stared at him.

"It ate at me all day. I decided to talk to him about it the next morning. I heard him leave early — around six. He'd told me he had to check on some work his crew had done in the park. So I got up and followed him there. He must have made a stop along the way, because I got there first. He was surprised to see me. Surprised and delighted. 'I love having my kid brother around' — that's what he said to me. 'You should visit more often, Fletcher.'" His eyes got watery.

Mrs. Blake touched his arm. "Fletcher — "

"I followed him to the bog. I said I wanted to take some pictures, and I did shoot a few. But really I was trying to get up my courage to talk to him. I even tried to convince myself that I must be wrong, that my brother would *never* do anything like that. But, Amanda, I *had* to ask him. I *had* to know. Finally, while he was checking the boardwalk, I did it. I asked him flat out if he'd run Matt off the road. You know what he said?"

Mrs. Blake stood as still as if she'd been turned to stone.

"He said no one but him had ever succeeded in getting you and no one was ever going to. At first I thought he was kidding. I reminded him that I'd met you first and that if I hadn't had that accident — "

Mrs. Blake gasped. "You can't think that Trevor was responsible for that. You told me yourself he

224

tried to stop you from diving off that embankment."

"I told you that because that's what Trevor told *me*. The truth is, I don't remember what happened. I'd been drinking. So I believed Trevor when he said he'd tried to stop me. Why wouldn't he? He was my big brother. He always looked out for me."

Mrs. Blake's head ticked from side to side again. "I don't believe it."

"He's my brother. I know him better than anyone. When I mentioned my accident, he got this look in his eyes. Just a look. So I asked him, 'It was an accident, right, Trev?' And he said, 'Would I lie to you?' Then I asked him again if he had anything to do with what happened to Matt."

"And?"

"And he repeated what he'd said — that no one had ever succeeded in getting you and that no one ever would." He looked down, just for a moment. When he raised his head, I could see pain in his eyes. He looked directly at Mrs. Blake. "I laughed," he said. "Can you believe that? I thought he was kidding and I laughed. Trevor laughed too. But I could see it in his eyes, Amanda. I could see it and I knew. He ran Matt off the road. He put me in a wheelchair. And I was lucky. I could have died."

Mrs. Blake stared at him.

"He turned and *walked* ahead of me on that boardwalk," Fletcher Blake said. "*Walked.*" He shook his head. "So easy for him — just to be able to walk. Me, I haven't walked in more than fifteen years. I'll never walk again. He walked. Then he knelt down.

And I — " He stared up at her. "I lost it. I reached for his hammer and grabbed it and . . . and I hit him."

"*You* killed Trevor?" Mrs. Blake's face was whiter than I had ever seen it. Her voice was a bare whisper when she said, "And I told you the police had questioned Matt. I told you they suspected him. What were you planning to do, Fletcher? Let them send Matt to prison? Because if you were, you're no better than Trevor."

Fletcher Blake's face went slack. "Amanda, no," he said. "I would never have done that. I would have said something. I almost told you this afternoon. If it had come to it, I'd have — "

"You'd have what, Fletcher?" Mrs. Blake said. "Look at what you've done already. We have to call the police. We have to tell them."

She stepped closer to him, so that he had to bend his neck to look up at her. He stared up at her for a moment. Then he did something I had never seen a grown man do before — he broke down and started to cry.

"I hit him," he said. "I could see he was dead. I didn't know what to do. And I was afraid of what you'd think. I panicked. I dumped him in the water. But I didn't want to hurt you, Amanda. I never wanted to hurt you."

My cell phone trilled again. Mrs. Blake handed me my purse and I fished my phone out with my good hand. It was Levesque, worried because he hadn't been able to reach me. I looked at Mrs.

226

Blake. She nodded. I told Levesque where I was.

Where before Mrs. Blake had been standing perfectly still, now she was shaking all over.

chapter 18

Dr. Bonnie Elliot confirmed it. My arm was broken. Which meant that Levesque had to drive me up to the hospital in Morrisville to have it set. He was on a pay phone almost the whole time we were sitting in the waiting room. He didn't tell me anything until after I had been X-rayed and my arm had been set. Then he took me to the Starbucks in the lobby of the hospital, where he bought himself a large coffee and me a genuine latte. We sat at a small table to drink them. I tried to ignore my throbbing arm.

"Fletcher Blake is under arrest," he said. "He made a full statement. David Mitchell has been released."

I started to cry. I couldn't help it. My arm hurt, I was tired and I had been so scared. I didn't want to be sitting there blubbering, but I couldn't stop myself.

Levesque got up and pulled a wad of napkins from a dispenser at the counter. The young guy behind the counter scowled at him. Levesque ignored him. He sat down and pressed the wad into my good hand. Then he put his arm around me, taking care not to put any pressure on my broken arm. He held it there until I stopped crying.

"I'm okay," I said.

"What did he do to you, Chloe?" He was talking softly but watching me intently. "And why?"

I told him what I'd wanted to tell him earlier in the evening — about Ross and his interview with Fletcher Blake, in which Fletcher had told Ross that he always left nature sites exactly as he had found them. He always picked up after himself. He also used the rakes and brushes that he carried in his van to carefully erase the tracks left by his wheelchair.

"He told Mrs. Blake that he didn't mean to kill his brother. He said that he lost it and hit Trevor and then panicked and dumped the body into the water."

"He must have decided to cover his tracks after that," Levesque said. "Kind of clear thinking for someone who'd panicked."

"I think he was more afraid of Mrs. Blake and Jessie finding out what he'd done than he was of you finding out," I said. "I think he's in love with Mrs. Blake."

Then I told him about how Fletcher Blake had talked Mr. Torelli into giving him Ross's interview tape. "He said he ruined it by accident, but I found it in the garbage."

"It was in his van. He told Steve he was going to destroy it after — " He broke off and looked hard at me.

"I'm fine," I said. Well, except for my arm. They'd given me something for the pain, but it didn't seem to be doing much good. "It was the picture that convinced me," I said. "It was taken in the park. It was a picture of the bog near where we found Trevor Blake."

Levesque frowned. "I don't understand."

"I'm pretty sure it was taken from right where we found the body. Fletcher Blake said that he shot a few pictures while he was finding the courage to bring up the subject of his accident with Trevor. The picture faced into the spruce bog. I recognized the sheep's laurel. That's the only place near here where it grows."

He waited for more.

"I was in the park the day before Adam and I found the body. Trevor Blake was there. His crew had just arrived to clean the place up. There was a lot to do. They couldn't have finished much before dark. The photo I saw — the one that Jessie had printed from Fletcher Blake's camera the day we found the body — it had been taken after the crew had cleaned the area up, but during the day. That means that it had to have been taken the morning Trevor Blake was killed. Which means that Fletcher Blake must have been in that part of the park that morning."

Levesque nodded. "I'm surprised he didn't delete it from his camera," he said.

"He showed up at Mrs. Blake's house at eight o'clock that morning. I remember thinking he looked tired, but that wasn't it. He had just killed his brother. He probably wasn't thinking straight. And he didn't have a chance to delete the picture, because Jessie grabbed his camera as soon as she saw him. She always does that, to see if he's taken any new pictures. When she saw the one of the bog, she ran inside and printed it. It was her favourite place to go with her father. Her uncle looked for the picture later, though. He was at Mrs. Blake's house when Jessie and I came back from town yesterday. He'd been looking through all of the pictures that Jessie had printed. He asked Jessie about it, but she said she'd destroyed it."

I glanced at the latte Levesque had ordered for me. Ordinarily, I'd have gulped it down by now. But I couldn't even make myself pick up the cup. All I wanted was for the pain to go away.

"I should take you home," Levesque said.

"No, it's okay. Finish your coffee."

He took a sip and frowned across the table at me.

"How did Fletcher know you had the photo?" he said.

"I don't think he did, at first. But he knew I'd found Ross's tape in the garbage. I told him I had put it back in there, but he must have checked and found that I hadn't. I think that's why he went into my purse — looking for the tape. I think he was surprised I had the photo."

"It must have spooked him. Once he knew you had the tape *and* the photo, he must have thought you'd put two and two together. And that you'd give them both to me. Where's the photo now?"

"He burned it. But Jessie has another copy. She printed one for her father. There's one thing I don't get, though. You said the killer was left-handed. As far as I can tell, Fletcher Blake isn't left-handed."

"No," Levesque said. "He isn't. But he's spent the past fifteen years in a wheelchair, so his arms are really strong. Also, he's used to grabbing hold of things with whichever hand is free. He just scooped up the hammer and swung."

"If Fletcher Blake killed his brother," I said slowly, "then those two men with Bryce Fuller must have been lying about what they saw in the park. I thought it was a little odd that they both happened to be in the park so early on a Sunday."

Levesque's expression was grim. "Bryce Fuller has a lot of influential friends. He used some of his contacts to get hold of confidential information on the investigation, then he used that information to try to make it appear that David Mitchell killed Trevor Blake."

"To get David Mitchell out of the way?" I said.

Levesque nodded and drained his coffee. "Come on," he said. "It's a long drive home. And it's late."

I didn't think it would be possible, because my arm hurt so much, but I fell asleep on the way home. The next thing I knew, Levesque was shaking me gently and helping me out of the car. I went to sleep with all my clothes on and woke up sore and fuzzy-headed. When I heard the doorbell, I squinted at the clock on my bedside table. It was afternoon. I got up and headed for the stairs. Levesque was standing at the front door. He turned when he heard me on the stairs.

"You have a visitor," he said.

It was Adam, clutching a bouquet of flowers. "Are you okay?" he said.

Levesque touched me on the shoulder and pulled me aside for a moment. "Don't be long, Chloe," he said. That's when I noticed the suitcase in the hall.

"You're leaving?"

"We both are."

"We? As in you and me?"

"Your mother doesn't want you here alone with a broken arm."

"So . . . what? You guys are taking me on your honeymoon?"

"We're taking you to Montreal. You're staying with Brynn until we come back."

"Aw, come on! I can look after myself."

"*I* know that," he said. "But your mother isn't so sure. And I am not going to have her spend one more minute of her vacation time worrying — about either of us. So do me a favour, say goodbye to your friend, get cleaned up and go pack a bag. If you need help, let me know."

I thought about arguing, but then decided he was right. Mom deserved a worry-free holiday. And I couldn't remember the last time that Brynn and I had spent time together. Besides, it turned out that Adam was going to be in town for the whole summer. He said he'd see me when I got back. He said, "By then I'll be desperate for someone to show me a good time. And Chloe? I want that someone to be you."

So did I.

After Adam left, I packed and then struggled downstairs with my suitcase. Levesque took it from me at the bottom of the stairs.

"You could have called me," he said. "You should be taking it easy."

I just shrugged.

"What about Jessie?" I said.

"Amanda Blake called this morning. I told her you were going to be away for a while. She understands. She and Jessie are going to take some time away too."

"That's not what I meant," I said. "How do you think Jessie is? First her father dies. Now this."

He shook his head. "We can stop by if you want."

"I'd like to." I had no idea what I was going to say to her, but it was the right thing to do.

Levesque was putting our suitcases into the car when a truck pulled into the driveway and David Mitchell got out. He approached our car, his eyes on me the whole time. Then he shifted to Levesque.

"Chief? I just want to thank you for, well, believing in me, I guess."

"I was just gathering all the facts," Levesque said. "Just doing my job."

David Mitchell looked at me. "I understand you didn't think I'd done it, either. Is that right?"

I shrugged. David Mitchell smiled.

"Like father, like daughter, huh?" he said. "I owe you an apology."

"You do?"

"That tree across the road? Turns out it was one of my guys. Emotions were running pretty high. I'm sorry."

I said it was okay.

After he'd gone, I said, "How does he know that I didn't think it was him?"

Levesque didn't answer.

"What about the golf course situation?" I said.

"What about it?"

"Aren't you afraid to leave things the way they are?"

Levesque shook his head. "Bryce Fuller has stopped construction for now."

"He has?"

"He has some more pressing matters to deal with."

"Like what?"

"Like criminal charges. He conspired with Lyle Turnbull and Maurice Dumont to make false statements to the police in a serious criminal matter. That's no joke."

"You think he'll go to jail?"

"A guy like Fuller can afford some pretty high-priced legal help," he said. "So . . . " He shrugged. "I don't know. But he made a statement first thing this morning. He's relocating the golf course. Maybe he thinks that will help him."

"Will it?"

"Not if I have anything to do with it. But with his money and connections . . . I think you can count on a lot of legal delays." He sounded disgusted.

"There's just one thing I don't understand," I said.

He waited.

"Jessie said her mother wasn't home the night Trevor Blake was killed. But Mrs. Blake told Jessie she was there."

I think Levesque smiled. It was hard to tell for sure.

"She was outside," he said.

"Outside?"

"With Matt Solnicki."

I frowned.

"Mrs. Blake doesn't believe in . . . " He stopped and thought for a moment. "She conducted her relationship with Matt Solnicki in private."

"I don't get it."

"They were in the tent," Levesque said. "She'd just agreed to marry him."

Oh.

"Get in the car. I promised your mother we'd be there tonight, which means we have to be on the road within the hour. But first we have to drop the dog at Jeanne's place and then stop by the Blakes'."

"And you don't want to break a promise to Mom, do you?"

"No," he said firmly. "I most certainly do not."

Watch for Book One of the
Robyn Hunter Mysteries,
coming in Spring 2006.

LAST CHANCE

All Robyn is doing at the animal rights demonstra-
tion is helping a friend avoid being arrested ... and
what happens? *She*'s the one the cops pick up. Her
mother manages to get the complainant to drop the
charges, but there's one condition: Robyn must vol-
unteer at the woman's favourite charity, an animal
shelter. For most people, that would be no punish-
ment at all. But for Robyn, who's terrified of dogs,
it's no picnic. To make matters even worse, Nick
D'Angelo works at the shelter — the very same guy
that she once caught stealing.

But has Nick changed? Maybe trying to rehabili-
tate problem dogs is helping him. ... Or maybe not.
It seems like Nick's in trouble again, and if Robyn
can't find out the truth, it could mean big trouble
for Nick ... and for the dog he's trying so desperately to save.

The Chloe and Levesque Series

The Third Degree
The book that launched the
Chloe and Levesque series.

Over the Edge
Can Chloe figure out who
. . . or what . . . pushed
Adam over the edge?

Double Cross
What *really* happened
to Jonah's mother?

Scared to Death
What is it that
has Tessa scared
to death?

Break and Enter
Someone is
setting Chloe up.

No Escape
Nobody but Chloe and
Phoebe believe Kyle's
brother is really innocent.

Not a Trace
There's no evidence of
who killed Trevor Blake
. . . not even a trace.

The Mike and Riel Series

Hit and Run
What's the real story
behind the hit and run
that killed Mike's mother?

Truth and Lies
One little lie leads to
another . . . until Mike
becomes a suspect in a
murder investigation.

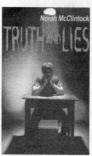

Dead and Gone
The discovery of a long-
buried body kick starts a
murder investigation that
has been unsolved for years.

Other McClintock Titles

Mistaken Identity
If Zanny's own father isn't
who she thought he was . . .
then who is *she?*

*The Body in
the Basement*
The body found in
Tasha's parents' café
is only the beginning.

Sins of the Father
What more can Mick do to
clear his father's name?

Password: Murder
Is it possible that
Harley really isn't
responsible for his
father's death?

Non-Fiction
by Norah McClintock

Body, Crime, Suspect
Investigating Crime Scenes
From the discovery of a body to the
verdict in court, find out how murder
cases are investigated.

Cover Photo Credits:
Left: First Light/A.G.E. Foto Stock/Bartomeu Amengual
Upper right and back cover: First Light/Rubberball
Lower right: First Light/A.G.E. Foto Stock/Bjorn Andren